LIAR LIAR

D'ARCO MAFIA DUET

JAYE PRATT

Copyright © 2023 by Jaye Pratt

All rights reserved. No part of this publication may be reproduced, stored or transmitted in any form or by any means, electronic, mechanical, photocopying, recording, scanning, or otherwise, without written permission from the publisher. It is illegal to copy this book, post it on a website, or distribute it by any other means without permission.

This novel is entirely a work of fiction. The names, characters, and incidents portrayed in it are the work of the author's imagination. Any resemblance to actual persons, living or dead, events or localities, is entirely coincidental.

Jaye Pratt asserts the moral right to be identified as the authors of this work.

Designations used by companies to distinguish their products are often claimed as trademarks. All brand names and product names used in this book and on its cover are trade names, service marks, trademarks and registered trademarks of their respective owners. The publishers and the book are not associated with any product or vendor mentioned in this book. None of the companies referenced within the book have endorsed the book.

Editing by Jenni Gauntt.

Blurb

They didn't come for me.

I wanted Killian to be the one to take my life, but five months later, nothing.

I'm still alive.

They promised they would follow me to the ends of the earth if I left.

They lied.

Now, I have no choice but to go back and clear my name.

I plan to walk in with my head held high and give them evidence that will force them into hearing me out. After all, Enzo gave me his word he would find my sister, and I want her back, no matter what the cost.

Killian and Sarge might be happy to see me back, but Enzo hasn't forgiven me for taking his mother's life, even if it was an accident, and she was the one behind hurting my sister.

Enzo can bite me. I'm back, and I know he won't let me leave, so I will be taking my rightful place as his wife.

Being back is not as easy as I expect when someone is working against us, long lost family resurfaces, mystery calls from someone who is supposed to be dead, and photographs of my best friend covered in blood. Whoever is behind this should have stayed hidden.

Friends become enemies, and enemies become allies; the tables have turned, and we all have to do what needs to be done to keep our family safe.

*To everyone who takes their future into their own hands.
Fuck the haters.*

AUTHOR NOTE

Please know this is a dark why choose mafia romance. It does come with a trigger warning which can be found on my website.

www.jayeprattauthor.com

Or feel free to reach out to me and I can send you a list.

Some content might be disturbing and may be traumatising to some readers. This book is on the lighter side of dark but some content may not be for everyone. If you have any triggers please head over to my website before starting.

Some scenes in this book have been dramatized to fit with the story and progress the storyline. Baby Mars is perfectly healthy, but he is born early, and I am aware that how quickly he is moved into his mother's room is not always the case.

PROLOGUE

MARIO

Running an empire worthy of my sons was a promise I made to my grandfather, God rest his soul. I'm a fair leader and do what needs to be done. I want my sons to follow in my footsteps. Enzo was made for this world; Angelo needs a firmer hand. He takes his lifestyle for granted. His mother babied him and always gave him what he wanted. I blame her for his softness. D'Arco men are not soft; we can't afford to be. The second we let our guard down, the vultures will swoop in and take everything we have worked hard for.

I might be many things, but I'm no idiot. Someone has been working against the family, and I plan to bring it all to light at the family meeting I have called. One of our own is a Fed. I can't say I'm all that surprised; Leo was a good kid, but his father was killed by my hand. A necessary means to an end. You can't talk to the Feds and expect that to come without consequences. He took his oath and dishonored it.

His son, Leo, being a Fed is not a tremendous deal. We can lead him to some small things, making his time undercover worthless. In the end, the kid will end up in a cell, and I will walk free. The issue at the current moment is the vermin in my inner circle, working against me, going against direct orders.

My own fucking wife and right-hand man—a bullet to the head would be too nice of a death.

Someone knocks at the door. "Come in," I huff.

Catalina struts into my office; she is going to make the perfect bride for my son. She has been promised to Enzo and will make a dutiful wife, trained in what is expected of her.

"You work too hard," she says, placing a cup of tea down in front of me. I huff. My doctor has told me to switch out the coffee in my diet.

"I have a family to run. People rely on me."

She takes a seat across from me and smiles. "You know Enzo would take more of the workload."

I pick up the tea, the quicker I drink it, the faster she will go away. Today is not the day I need her here, getting in the way. I love the girl like my own daughter, she just needs to not be around when shit hits the fan. I need to get everything ready for tomorrow, have all my ducks in a row, so to speak. My wife is a smart woman, and I don't need to alert her to what I know.

"I know, he works too hard," I say, standing from my chair, and a wave of dizziness has me fall back into my chair as a cold sweat breaks out over my body. Catalina rushes to my side.

"Mario, are you okay?"

"I don't know, my chest burns," I gasp. Something isn't right.

"I will call 911," she says. I can't argue with her, something isn't right.

I try to keep calm, there is no fucking way I'm having a heart attack. I was healthy as an ox at my last checkup.

Paramedics arrive and fire off questions. The shortness of breath makes it hard to answer, but Catalina stands with me and holds my hand as they load me into an ambulance. The doors closing are the last thing I remember.

Blinking my eyes open, memories of the day I had my heart attack, or supposed heart attack, flood back. Days blurred into weeks, and I no longer know how long I have been locked up. What I do know is my wife is behind it all.

The stupid cunt has locked me in the bomb shelter I purchased for us back when all the buzz was around about the end of the world. Except she has locked all the exits.

I have everything I need down here, though, I'm not sure why she even keeps me alive. Killing me would be an easier option, so she must need me. I'm taking a wild guess that she needs me to take the fall for the trafficking ring. Aldo came to me with the figures; they both did, but I wouldn't budge. My own fucking sister was taken as a girl, so they may as well have spat in my face, insulting me that way.

I have tried breaking out numerous times, but the bunker was made to withstand everything. End of the world and all that. They have a fucking metal shock collar around my neck, the only sign that someone is coming. It keeps me down long enough, so I can't kill them.

Elena and Aldo can't be the only ones involved, but so

far, they are the only ones who have shown their faces, and it's only a matter of time before I find a way out.

The sound of a car pulling up has me bracing for the shock, but as the footsteps get closer, it doesn't come.

"Help! I'm down here," I yell, banging against anything that will make noise.

"Mario."

Leo! Great, the fucking Feds are here to arrest me. I figured this day would come. At least in prison, I can find a way to get a message to my son.

Leo steps inside the first door of the bunker. "I would say it's good to see you, kid, but being arrested for a crime I didn't commit..."

"I know it wasn't you, it took me long enough to figure it out," he says, and he tries different keys to open the secondary bars that separate us. "Elena and Aldo are the ones. I fucked up, and I'm sorry, but so much has happened. Your daughter-in-law is going to need your help. She is pregnant with Enzo's baby, but she killed your wife...by accident."

"And Enzo is going to kill her. He doesn't know his mother is involved."

Leo shakes his head no. "He will shortly. Jordyn has gone back with the evidence."

"Jordyn?" I question with a raised brow. Every time Elena comes here, she yaps on and on about Catalina.

"Long story, Enzo won't marry Cat; she screwed Angelo. He took matters into his own hands."

I nod. "And you?"

Leo looks up at me and swallows hard. "I'm running before he kills me, but I couldn't leave you here to rot. I should have left everything for the family to deal with. For that, I'm sorry, and I'm sorry for thinking the worst of you. I found a tape, one hidden from evidence. My father, he..."

"Was a rat, I know. He accepted what had to happen and made me promise to look after you. A promise I will keep until I'm dead."

His eyes go wide, shock visible on his features. He came here knowing that it was a possibility I would kill him. He hands me the keys; hopefully one takes off this damn collar. I grab his arm and pull him into a hug. "Go, live your life. I will make sure my son knows your debt to us is clear. You understand that means you can never come back here."

Leo nods. "Thank you. I have to hide; the Feds will be looking for me."

Once Leo leaves, I try the small keys on the collar, and lucky for me, my wife kept everything on one key ring. I don't know how Leo got hold of them, but now I plan to wait. I told Leo as much. He gave me his gun. Aldo will be here any time now. Someone always comes to bring me fresh water and supplies.

I don't have to wait long at all. I'm surprised because Elena had only visited a day or two ago. The collar fucking buzzes from the metal table, and I smirk when it stops. I grab it, moving out from behind the bars and into the small space between the entry and behind the door. It opens inwards, so he won't see me until it's too late.

The door opens, and I wait, one step, two, and the door starts to close. Fuck, it's not Aldo unless he is now a six-foot-six brick shit-house Russian. I don't give him a chance, just a smack to the side of the head that makes him sidestep and feel disorientated for a split second. Long enough to press the barrel to his head. He holds up his hands, and I wrap the metal collar around his thick neck.

"Hand over the clicker," I demand. "And don't try anything stupid."

He does as I ask, and I shock the fucker until he drops, patting him down before removing all his weapons.

I'm thankful that when I push the door open, a nice-sized rock sits by the entry. I don't want to bash him over the head with it, but Killian needs to get his hands on this man, and I guess this means we are going to war with the Bratva.

Ivan might not be involved—he is a man of his word—but Lev; he has just proven why we can't trust anyone. Fuck, my own wife and closest friend worked against me.

With a lot of sweating and muscle, I manage to get Lev into the trunk, and lucky for me, he keeps rope and cable ties in his SUV. How convenient.

Fuck Aldo, that fool will get word that I'm alive and run. I will find him and deal with him later. Even if I spend the rest of my life hunting him down. He will forever be watching his back.

Now it's time to go and see my sons and meet the woman who holds the future heir to the D'Arco family.

CHAPTER ONE

ENZO

My entire world, in a matter of minutes, has been thrown upside down. Jordyn stands in front of me with a round belly that holds my child. My father has walked through the door dragging Lev behind him. Kill is the first to move toward my father, doing as he asks, and starts dragging the giant Russian through the foyer. Sarge moves toward Jordyn, but she holds her hand out to stop him. He shakes his head and storms from the room.

The pain in my chest squeezes behind my ribs, making it hard to breathe. What the fuck is happening to me, it feels like I'm dying?

"Son," my father says, taking a step toward me and I pull my gun aiming it his way. My father has never been afraid of death; he looks me directly in the eyes and takes a step forward.

"How are you alive?"

My chest rises and falls in rapid succession, and my

nostrils flare in anger. I must be going crazy, that has to be it. In all my thirty years of life, I have never felt so confused.

"How about we put the weapon down, and I will explain everything?"

I nod, and he reaches out and takes the gun from my shaking hands.

"I'm going to see my sister," Jordyn says, not waiting for a reply. She heads up to Angelo's old wing, where I have set her up a room and her nanny, a trained therapist. A girl her age doesn't need to be sleeping amongst men; I wanted her to feel safe and secure. We don't know what the kid went through, but if the screams at night are anything to go by, it wasn't pretty. I watch her walk up the stairs and turn back to my father, who leads us into the sitting room. I follow behind him in a daze.

He starts by explaining the day I thought he died, the pains in his chest, and blacking out when he got into the ambulance. When he came to, he was locked in the family bunker, one I had very limited knowledge of. Yes, I knew it existed, but a doomsday bunker was not a place I ever cared to visit. I had no reason to unless the world was ending.

He goes on to tell me how my mother and Aldo wanted to get into the sex trade, and he refused, so he was planning on outing them to the family, but they beat him to it, planning his death.

The information swirls around in my head, running my hands through my hair, my head pounds with all the details.

"What do we do now?" I ask when he finishes.

"First step is you calling Aldo, hoping he doesn't know I'm missing from the bunker yet, then we reinforce this house. We are going to war, and it will not end well, son."

I nod as my father stands. "I'm not back to take your place. While I was 'dead,' I realized it was almost a relief not being in charge. I'm going to be the best Nonno to my grandchild, and once you're not in shock, I would like you to fill me in on everything I have missed."

Again, I nod; what else can I do? My father excuses himself, says he has some calls to make. I pull out my own cell and dial Aldo, but the call goes straight to voicemail.

Sarge comes into the room, his eyes rimmed red. I don't comment on it; we are all in as much shock as each other.

"I need you to move Lev's car. Aldo was working against the family and my father has me trying to contact him."

Sarge doesn't respond, he just turns and leaves the room. Loosening my tie, I head upstairs. I need a shower or a nap because right now, I'm numb to everything. I was in charge a little over a year, and I epically fucked up. My father was alive, Leo was a Fed, and my wife killed my mother, who was selling young girls. I don't deserve the title as head of this family, and while my father says he doesn't want it back, he needs to take it. We are going to war with a crime family that could easily match us in manpower. The only man who could possibly diffuse the situation just wants to be a Nonno to a baby I didn't want with a woman I barely know.

Upstairs in my room, I don't remember walking up the stairs or starting the shower, but the water feels nice cascading over my body.

"So, you're going to be a dad."

I look up and see Sarge leaning against the counter. "I'm sorry," I whisper to him. I know he and Missy had spoken about starting a family. This is something he wanted so badly. I fall to my knees with my head in my hands.

I'm not weak; D'Arco men don't cry. Strong arms wrap around me. "You're not weak, you're the strongest man I know. You just found out that your father is alive, and your wife is carrying your child, you're human."

Moving my head up, my eyes connect with his, and I nod. "Here is what is going to happen, let it all out, then you can get dressed and talk to Jordyn."

"I can't talk to her," I whisper. Sarge stands and helps me to my feet; he is still fully clothed, dripping with water.

"You can. Do you want her to take her sister and run?"

I shrug. "Maybe she should. I wanted her dead, and if it weren't for the Feds being up my ass, I would have made Kill slowly torture her to death. Would I have even known she was pregnant? I could have killed my child. I'm a monster and don't deserve a child."

Sarge pushes against my chest, my back hitting the tiles with a hard thump, his eyes zero in on my lips before his mouth smashes against mine.

A war has been brewing between us for years, neither of us acting on it. The intensity of his kiss grounds me, and primal nature takes over. My hand wraps around the back of his neck, and my tongue forces entry into his mouth, dominating the kiss, just like the way I dominate in life. He pulls back, and I pant, dizzy with need. Sarge leans in and presses a light kiss against my shoulder as he looks up at me, and I nod. His kisses travel down my pecs and over my abs as he lowers himself to the ground.

A man has never had his lips wrapped around my cock before, but Sarge isn't any man, he is my right-hand man whether he likes it or not. The man who would take a bullet for me and protect me with his life. My teeth grind together, and my hand grips his hair as he takes my cock inch by inch into the back of his throat. The deeper he takes me, the more my eyes roll back into my head. When I look back down at him, he has my entire fucking length down his throat. I pull back and then thrust forward, testing how much he can take. That's what he wants me to do right now, use him and get my power back. My hand wraps tighter around his hair, and my thrusts become harder, using my best friend until I see stars and come down his throat.

When he pulls back and looks up at me, everything has changed, and he knows it. I pull him up and suck his bottom lip into my mouth, biting down before I let go.

"Mine," I growl possessively. He just smirks at me and steps out of the shower, stripping off his clothes and wrapping my towel around his waist. It's then I spot Jordyn standing at the door with her arms crossed and a sour look on her face.

Sarge freezes, and when she doesn't look his way, he walks past her. She can't just fucking ignore the one man in this house that was willing to go to fucking war with me and turn his back on this life to run away with her sister and hunt her ass down. I might have had a moment of weakness, but now I'm back, and it's time I do what I was born to do. Run this family. She better get on board really fucking quickly, or the last thing she will do on this earth will be an incubator for my child.

She doesn't move as I step out of the shower, and her eyes don't roam over me as they once did. I let the water drip from my body since Sarge took my towel, and I walk past her and into my room, knowing she will follow behind me.

CHAPTER TWO

JORDYN

Pixie being alive was all I have thought about for the five months I was gone. I thought she had been sold and that I would never see her again. When Killian didn't come for me, I planned out a way to take my life; the guilt ate at me day in and day out. When the vomiting started, I had presumed that it was from stress.

The day I was ready, I waited for Leo to go into town to meet his boss. I found some rope days prior and attached it to a beam inside the old barn, no longer able to walk the earth. They say when you're about to die, your life flashes before your eyes, but there was nothing but a deep black abyss of nothingness when I let myself fall. When the rope bit into my skin and tightened, I just closed my eyes and let it take over. That was until Leo came back because he was only picking up a delivery that day. He cut me down, took me back into the house, and shoved a pregnancy test box into my hands.

I laughed at him. There was no way I was pregnant; I

had been on birth control since I became a teenager. Still, he insisted I take it to humor him. When the two lines came up thick and fast, I wanted to die even more. I didn't want a baby. Life has a cruel way of punishing people, and for whatever reason, the three possible fathers all wanted me dead, or at least I thought they did until none of them showed up. Maybe I really meant that little to them.

I spiraled into a depression I wasn't prepared for, and if it wasn't for Leo, I may have gone through with my plans. Somehow, day by day, he convinced me that Pixie's memory would live on through my child. He even organized the DNA test, and when it came back that it was Enzo's child, he explained the immunity clause within the D'Arco family.

However, I still had my doubts... What good is immunity if they took the baby and then killed me? But that isn't how it works. Which I didn't know until the day he came back with a stack of papers, tears in his eyes, and explained that he found the files on his father, ones that detailed his ratting out Mario, his lifelong friend, to buy his own freedom. He also had a picture of Pixie with Sarge, and my heart stopped. That is when I knew I had to go back and get her, but the second I was back, I needed to use the power I had.

The D'Arco family was behind my sister going missing, and I'm staying until everyone involved gets what they deserve. Even if that means I become a prisoner in this fucking house.

I followed Pixie up to her room. My damn heart melted when I noticed they had transformed the room just for her. As it was, holding her in my arms didn't feel real. We both cried until some woman knocked on the door and told Pix it was time for her therapy session.

"What do you want, Jordyn? I have shit to do," Enzo snaps. How dare he be angry at me. He had my sister and knew where I was.

"Were you ever planning to tell me?"

He scoffs at me. "Pot calling the kettle black, don't you think?"

I follow his movements around the room. He wants me to comment on him and Sarge, and I won't, no matter how hot it was to watch.

"You knew how much finding her meant to me, and you knew where I was the whole fucking time."

He crosses the room in a blink of an eye and wraps his hand around my throat, forcing me backward until my back slams against a wall, knocking the air from my lungs.

"I wanted to come for you, to bring you back here and show you your sister's face one last time before I let Kill have his way with you."

Tears run down my face. "So why didn't you? I was waiting."

That stuns him slightly. His grip on my neck is loose, and as much as he wants to steal the air from my lungs, he wouldn't hurt a child, something I knew all along.

"Because Kill didn't give me your location. He wanted to wait until the Feds were off our ass, and Sarge was a loose cannon, ready to kill us all. They bought you time."

Swiping his hand from my neck, he lets it drop easily. I push forward and slam my hands against his chest. "You don't get it! I didn't want to be saved." I scream. "All I wanted to do was die. Living with the nightmares of what happened to my sister was a fate worse than death, and you all fucking knew that. You promised you would come for me if I ever ran, and you didn't come... You didn't come!"

Enzo shocks me and steps forward, wrapping his arms around me. I try to fight him to let me go, hitting him in the chest with clenched fists, but he just holds me close until I get it all out. When I'm done, he pulls me in tighter.

"You might be safe for now, but I won't forget that you killed my mother."

He pushes me away, and the pure hatred burns right through me. "You want a war with me, Mr. D'Arco, then bring it. She was a vile piece of shit, and the second I found out she was the one behind selling my sister, I was glad I did it. I hope she rots in fucking hell!"

"Get the fuck out!" he bellows. I flip him off, exiting his room, and head back downstairs. That's one down and two to go. Killian will be in the basement.

Opening the door, I follow the stairs down to a secondary door and swing it open. They chained the massive guy up, and I'm surprised it's not Killian I see, it's Mario. He has freshly showered and has his shirtsleeves rolled to his elbows. His head turns slightly as I walk through the door.

"Bella Ragazza, this is no place for you to be."

I smile at the man, and the hairs on the back of my neck prickle. "This is the exact right spot for my woman," Killian says, and Mario's brows dip.

"I'm not your woman," I say, turning to face him. "Not when you didn't come for me."

Killian chuckles.

"I think I might check if they have found my bastard right-hand man. He needs to explain himself," Mario says as he leaves the room.

"You wanted me to come for you?" Killian asks, and I nod.

"Every fucking day. The hatred of myself festered inside of me, and I wanted it to stop. You could have made it all go away."

He reaches up and runs a finger down my jaw. "Awe, Poppet, I'm honored that you wanted it to be me. I would have done it, you know that. Little worm, however, made me promise to get you back."

"Little worm?"

"Your sister. She is so much like you, and Sarge had to go and make nice with her. The kid even has Enzo wrapped around her little finger. She wanted you back, and I can't say I didn't agree, even if having you in chains again would have been a wet dream."

"You still should have come for me; did I mean that little to you?"

He leans forward, and I can feel his breath against my lips. "Don't you see? If I came for you and Enzo forced my hand, Sarge would have killed Enzo, his best friend, and then I would have had to kill Sarge, which would have left me to raise a teenage girl. They broke her, Poppet, and she doesn't need the likes of me teaching her how to become a woman."

Fuck him and his rational thinking. I just want to...to... punch him in the throat, so I do, and he fucking laughs.

"Fuck you, Killian," I snap, turning my back to him.

"All you have to do is ask, Poppet!" he yells out as my foot hits the first step. Motherfucker.

I'm not ready to face Sarge, yet. I know he wouldn't have wanted me dead. He is a man of reason, the one I am glad was watching over my sister.

CHAPTER THREE

SARGE

Enzo comes downstairs, but I can't meet his eyes. I know what we did upstairs changes things. Enzo is very possessive, and I wanted that, but Jordyn being back also changes things. Surely, he won't just forget that I would have left him for her. She was the game changer in my life, opening my eyes that I could feel again.

"Aldo isn't answering," Enzo says. "My uncles are also on their way." Meeting his eyes, I nod and wait. Mario won't be far, either.

A car on the gravel crunches and stops close to the front stairs. Angelo bursts through the doors, frantically looking around.

"Papa!"

"Son," Mario says, stepping into the room and Angelo runs into his father's arms. Mario's two brothers are standing there with smiles on their faces. No matter the situation, Giovanni and Roberto always look happy.

"Look who is still alive, I knew it would take more than a

heart attack to take you down," Roberto says with a laugh as he steps through the door.

"I think it's time we went and had a little chat," Mario says to his brothers.

The older men all start to move out of the foyer and Enzo goes to follow, but his father stops him. "Give me a minute alone with them, maybe feed your wife. She looks very skinny."

I whip my head to where Jordyn stands. She does look like she has lost weight, even with the small bump she has. If Leo wasn't feeding her, then I would personally hunt him down and kill him myself.

Enzo slightly turns his head to look at Jordyn, just enough that she can't see, but I do. "Also, gather the family, it's time we celebrate my return. I want to officially meet your wife."

Enzo nods, and his father turns around and follows behind his brothers.

"Kitchen," Enzo demands, and Jordyn almost looks like she wants to argue but thinks better of it.

I follow behind them; I have so many things that I want to say but also nothing at all. Enzo starts pulling containers out of the refrigerator, and Kill walks in.

"Well, that is the first time someone has ever kicked me out of my basement."

Kill gravitates toward Jordyn and takes a seat beside her. Grabbing her stool, he pulls her towards him. I wish I could, but I'm still so fucking mad at her because she left us and at myself for not going after her, protecting her. That is what it all boils down to. I lost Missy, and as mad as Enzo was after he found out she killed his mother, I know he wouldn't have killed her, I wouldn't have let him. I may not have been able to protect her from the Feds or Enzo's mother, but I would have protected her from him.

I take a seat on the stool next to Kill, and he doesn't pay any attention to me. Enzo is the first to break the silence.

"Let's cut the shit, yeah? You're sure the baby is mine?"

Jordyn looks up at him. "No, I'm just saying it for shits and giggles."

Enzo's jaw goes tight. "How the fuck am I supposed to trust you, Doll? The cops said you ratted us out, and I believed you, but then I watched video evidence of you killing my flesh and blood and leaving with the rat."

"That rat had seen me accidentally murder a woman, so excuse fucking me if I thought I better do as he asks, and why I did was for a few reasons. Selfishly, I didn't want to go to prison, and I thought maybe while I waited for you assholes to find me and kill me, I could make him look deeper into who was involved in the trafficking because all of this," she says waving her hands manically around in the air, "all stems from me doing whatever it takes to find Pixie. I was honest about that from the day we met. For a smart man, Enzo, you're a fucking idiot."

Killian snorts from beside her. "Poppet, let's not push it, there are going to be enough murders here today."

"As mad at you all as I am, I should have at least said thank you for looking after Pixie."

A part of me breaks down at her sincerity. I know being mad is a reflection on myself for not being there for her, but I would protect her sister at all costs. I know how much she means to her.

"Why are you thanking him?" Pixie asks as she bounces

into the kitchen. The girl hides her trauma very well, the same way Jordyn does. "He is a dickhead."

Enzo swears under his breath in Italian, and Pixie chuckles, "I can understand you, you know. You can call me a spoiled brat all you like, but whose name is on the credit card I have?"

Pixie stands beside Jordyn and puts her hand on her stomach. "I hope my nephew is nothing like you."

Enzo's eyes widen. I think this is the first time he has realized or acknowledged that the baby is a boy.

"Don't be so hasty, young one, my son is a fine man when he pulls the stick out of his ass," Mario says, coming into the kitchen. "And who might you be? I wasn't aware there would be two beautiful women upon my return."

"Pixie Rae, and I'm sorry you are related to him."

Mario bellows out a laugh. "I think I like you."

"The jury is still out on you since you have the same blood."

Mario gets closer to Jordyn, and the room gets tense. Killian's hand grasps her leg, and I see her wince.

He offers Jordyn his hand. "We haven't officially met, it's a pleasure to meet you."

Jordyn takes his hand, and Mario places a kiss on her skin, and Killian growls under his breath. Mario doesn't bat an eyelid, just bends slightly. "And my grandson, may I?"

He peers back up at Jordyn, and she nods. He places both of his hands on her stomach, and he laughs. "Was that?"

Jordyn smiles back at him and nods her head. "Leo felt him move for the first time the other day."

Enzo slams a cup down onto the counter, and it shatters. Pixie screams at the loud noise, and Mario jumps to his feet to pull her into his arms. He talks really fast in Italian, telling Enzo that he needs to calm down. Pixie relaxes in Mario's arms, and Jordyn's brows furrow. I know she wishes her sister jumped to her for support, but she just doesn't know Mario well enough to know that people are naturally drawn to him.

"I have given Leo a pardon. He is to never come back here, but he saved my life. When he explained he had an inkling after he started looking into your mother, which led him to Aldo and tracking his phone. He was curious why he was visiting the bunker."

"You what?" Enzo booms.

"Now is not the time. We can argue about this later. Right now, I want you to call the family doctor. I want to make sure that my grandson is healthy, and I want to get to know my daughter-in-law and the little firecracker. Where is the cook? We need some food."

Enzo is pissed, but he doesn't push his father. He stands back and watches Mario and Jordyn chat. Pixie joins in the conversation, and all three of us just sit and watch how easily she has won him over.

CHAPTER FOUR

JORDYN

Mario has called a family meeting; Enzo was furious when he found out his father had invited me. At first, I was going to turn him down purely so I could spend some alone time with Pixie. I don't like the thought of her being alone.

Mario assured me that the property now has double security, and Pixie has her own personal security. Which eases my discomfort on leaving, which I will because Enzo doesn't want me to, and I will not make being back easy on him.

Finding clothes to wear from my old wardrobe isn't easy with a bump. I opted for a black cotton dress with a small slit up the side, a denim jacket, and a white pair of tennis shoes. My hair has grown out, and being pregnant, I don't want to do much with it until he is born. I curl it and put in a little spray so it holds.

"Are you ready?" Killian asks, popping his head into my room. I nod, grabbing my handbag off the bed. I never used to take a bag everywhere I went, but now they make good snack holders.

Killian doesn't speak as I follow him down to the foyer, where everyone else is waiting.

"O.M.G," Charlotte says, followed by a squeal, and she rushes towards me, her hands going straight to my stomach. "Why didn't you tell me?"

She throws a stink eye at Enzo.

"Wasn't sure it was mine," Enzo snaps, and I flip him off.

"My sister isn't a liar, unlike you."

Pixie skips down the stairs of Angelo's wing in a set of PJs that look the exact same as what Charlotte is wearing. She must notice the way I look between them.

"Girls' night," Charlotte explains, and I nod.

"Are you sure that you are okay with me leaving?" I ask my sister, and she rolls her eyes at me.

"I'm not a baby anymore, and Charlotte looks after me all the time."

A pang of guilt hits me in the heart. I'm grateful that she has had people looking out for her, but it should have been me.

Mario steps into the room; he has the silver fox thing going for him, and he is built. Good for him.

"Stop drooling over Enzo's father, or I might have to kill him, Poppet."

I snort. "You three old men are enough for me."

Killian chuckles from behind me, and fuck if I didn't miss the sound of his voice. It's irrational that I haven't forgiven him for not coming and killing me, considering that Pixie is alive, but I feel betrayed. He told me he would hunt me down if I left, and he didn't. What sort of bullshit is that?

Mario leads the way out to the SUV. Mario insists I ride shotgun next to Sarge, who still won't look me in the eye. I know we need to sit down and talk. He feels betrayed, and that won't be an easy fix. I think I'm the most grateful to him, his deep-rooted grief saved my life and my baby.

Even thinking about being a mother scares the life out of me, bringing an innocent soul into this fucked up world. Yet I didn't have the heart to have an abortion. Part of this baby is also a part of Pixie, in a weird way. Leo had an entire speech about family, but I never had one of those. I had my sister, and he argued that meant I had family. Fuck him and his logic. It's weird that I miss our chats. I know what he did to the D'Arco family was a shit move, but in the end, he did the right thing, or maybe what he did was fucking stupid and against the law, depending on who you ask.

Nervous energy fills the car, and I wonder how this is all going to play out with Mario back and just surprising his entire family. It will save him hours calling everyone. I have seen the amount of immediate family members there are.

Enzo organized the meeting to be at the club. With Mario back and knowing there could be more family members involved in trying to take them down, they need to be careful.

Sarge drives down into the underground parking, and he is the first to exit the car, followed by the men in the second SUV. They clear the area, and the rest of us get out.

Mario puts his hand on Sarge's shoulder. "Boy, you need to take a step back and let the men do their jobs. You need to decide tonight if you are replacing Aldo. We need to be a solid unit, and you know there is no one better to calm my son and make him see reason."

Sarge nods, and I see his eyes well with tears. Mario's words obviously mean a lot to him. "I'll do it. Someone has to make sure he doesn't get killed before the baby comes."

Mario's smile takes over his face, and he nods.

"Kaser, it's on you to head up security."

The man, who looks to be in his early forties, nods and starts directing his men. We all walk in unison toward the elevator; Mario presses the button, and my stomach already does flips. As we step inside, Sarge slips his hand in mine and gives it a squeeze, and my stupid heart does backflips. There is no way I could ever be mad at this man, not when he remembers the little things.

Martha gives Enzo a wave as we exit the elevator, her eyes go wide, and Mario chuckles. Once we get to the function room, Kaser pushes the door open, and the chatter dies down the second Enzo walks through the door. A loud scream pierces the air, and one of Enzo's aunts faints.

"Did you miss me?" Mario announces to the room. It's like a free-for-all, men and women rush toward us. Killian and Sarge flank me and move me away from the stampede of people. This is worse than when the doors open for a black Friday sale.

After a few minutes, Mario asks everyone to step back and quiet down. He goes on to explain what happened to him, and the crowd is stunned silent, only gasps from an aunt can be heard. Once he is done, he asks if anyone has questions.

"Are you taking back your position in the family?" someone in the back asks.

"No, Enzo has been doing a fine job. I have other things I plan to do with my time."

The old guy grumbles, clearly not Enzo's biggest fan. I watch as Sarge reaches out and places his hand on Enzo's shoulder, and he visibly relaxes.

"Is anyone else in the family involved?" one of Enzo's aunts asks.

"Right now, I don't know. I called this meeting hoping if anyone else is, they would be smart enough to run because Enzo will find them, and Killian has some special treatment for those who dishonored the family."

Everyone looks toward Killian, and some even visibly shudder. He drops his head, hiding behind the safety of his hoodie.

"Who is the bitch pregnant by? We all know she fucks the three of them."

My mouth falls open when Angelo gets out of his seat and grabs Cat around the back of the neck. "You will not disrespect my brother's wife. I fucked up royally and want to offer my apology to Jordyn for my behavior."

Cat scoffs as Angelo drags her toward where Enzo and Mario stand. He pushes her, and she trips, landing on her hands and knees in front of Enzo, who leans down and takes her chin, forcing her to look up at him.

"Don't force me to kill you. Our friendship goes back decades, but you disrespect my wife or question that the baby is not mine. I won't hesitate to end you. This is your last warning; I suggest you heed it."

Tears run down her face. I don't miss the smirk, and her head drops; that bitch is playing with fire. She pretends to compose herself.

"I'm sorry. I should not have said what I did. My entire life, I always imagined I would carry your child, and I let jealousy get the better of me. Pixie coming into this family is a blessing, she is an amazing young girl. Everyone loves her so much."

The hairs on the back of my neck stand on end, and my jaw goes hard as I slice my gaze to Enzo. His warning glare is just that, a warning not to start. I bite down hard on my tongue, the tang of blood welcomed. He let that cunt near my sister.

"Who is replacing Aldo?" someone shouts, diverting Enzo's attention from me as Angelo drags Cat away.

"Sergeant will step up effective immediately. My father has invited him to take Aldo's place, and he will take the oath tonight. I expect everyone that needs to be there will be present."

A few men nod, and then Enzo comes to my side and takes my hand. I walk by his side and pretend that we are good to save face, but we are far from it. Everyone wants to ask us questions—how far along I am, have we picked a name? Enzo's aunt, Rosa, goes into detail about the tradition in the D'Arco family. Enzo was named after his grandfather, just like all the first sons in the family. I don't know how I feel about my son being named Mario; I have nothing against the name, but I would like to have the option to name my child.

CHAPTER FIVE

JORDYN

Enzo has enforced the *us sleeping in the same room* rule, and to say I'm pissed is the understatement of the century. The housekeeper helped me find some spare pillows while Enzo took a business call in his office. Like a salty teenager, I build a wall of pillows to separate the king bed. Once I'm done, I have worked up a sweat and flop down onto my side. Doing shit with a stomach is hard work. I don't understand why anyone would willingly do this repeatedly. Hats off to them because it's hard work.

Enzo strides through the door and doesn't acknowledge me or even look my way; he loosens his tie and heads straight for the ensuite.

While he is in there, I quickly get changed into an oversized shirt I pinched from Sarge's room. Once I'm tucked into bed scrolling on my phone, Enzo opens the ensuite door and steam billows out, followed by my asshole husband, who looks like a damn snack in the light gray cotton pajamas that hang low on his hips. Fuck him. Before I left, they spoiled me in the orgasm department, and going without all these months has me horny as fuck. He knows I'm watching him, or more so his cock, as he walks toward the bed. I'm his wife, and I can look all I want.

He slips into the bed, and I roll to my side away from him. "Don't you think the pillows are a little juvenile?"

I roll onto my other side. "Excuse me, juvenile? I don't want to touch you. You are an asshole, and you have the nerve to be pissed at me."

His scent wafts toward me, and my fucking mouth waters. "I'm not pissed at you, Doll. I'm fucking livid. You killed my mother."

I scoff. Are we back to this? Flashes of her lifeless body have me rolling away from him. I won't keep explaining myself. Killian was right, though, killing someone changes you.

Closing my eyes, I let the tears roll down my face. If I could go back, I would have tried harder to see if she had a gun, because I swear, she did.

"Ugh," I whisper as the baby moves like an acrobat inside my stomach.

"Are you okay?" Enzo asks, leaning over the pillow wall. I nod but don't look at him. I really don't want him to see me crying.

"Just the baby kicking, it's getting harder every day. Did you want to feel?"

"Sure," he says and slides his hand over my stomach. I place mine on top of his, moving it to where he is kicking.

"Fuck, was that?" he asks, and I nod.

Enzo doesn't rush to move his hand, and at some point, my eyes start to get heavy, and I fall asleep.

Enzo's hand rests on my stomach, mine covering his, and I must be feeling brave because I slide it down beneath the top of my cotton panties. I guide his finger to my clit and help him rub circles on my nub. Wetness pools between my thighs. It's been so long since Enzo has touched me, and I want him to climb on top of me and slowly thrust inside me so I can savor the feeling of his cock.

A moan slips from my lips as a wave of pleasure hits my core. He buries two fingers inside me before my orgasm finishes.

"Fuck, you're beautiful when you come."

Blinking my eyes open, I realize that I'm not dreaming. Enzo pulls his fingers out of me and brings them to his mouth.

"You're a fucking asshole," I snap, whacking him in the chest with the back of my hand. "You knew I was dreaming."

"Did I, Doll? You moved my hand between your legs."

Throwing the blanket off, I slide out of bed and stomp to the bathroom. My underwear is soaked through, and I consider going to find Killian, but I think better of it. He is still a man who is unstable, and I can't risk him cutting my fucking head off while I'm pregnant.

"Jordyn," Pixie calls from in the bedroom.

"Do you know how to knock?" Enzo asks her.

"Do you know how to not be a dickhead...didn't think so."

She busts through the door and closes it behind herself. "Can I go to the mall with my friends today?"

The door opens again while I'm still sitting on the fucking toilet. Enzo turns on the faucet and washes his hands and picks up his toothbrush.

"You can't go to the mall."

Pixie's head whips to him. "You're not my dad, you can't tell me what to do."

Enzo levels her with a glare, but she doesn't cower. "No, I'm not your father, you don't fucking have one. You might hate me, and that's fine, but right now, we are going to war, and you and your sister are easy fucking targets. You will stay in this house..."

"Or what?" she pushes.

"I will take you down to the basement and lock your ass up until it's safe."

"I fucking hate you!" Pixie screams and storms out of the room.

I try not to laugh because Enzo is pissed. The vein on the side of his head pulsates every time he is pissed off.

"Is that what it's like to be a parent? Because if it is, I don't know if it's for me."

I laugh; I can't help it. A preteen girl is not an easy species to navigate, and the men in the house have been thrown into the deep end.

"How would I know? I was nine when Pix was born, and I remember her being cute, and she cried a lot."

I wipe and flush. Enzo avoids eye contact while I do it, which I'm grateful for. I move next to him as he brushes his teeth and wash my hands before getting my toothbrush out. We stand side by side in silence, but only one thing stands out. This all seems a little too domesticated for my liking.

The last few days have gone by in a blur. The men are rarely here, and now that Pixie is back, I don't care all that much about what they are doing. Kaser, head of security, has a team here at the house, and he showed me where the safe room is and how to access it in case of an emergency.

Sarge is still avoiding me, even though I know he is secretly happy to see me back. Enzo, I would say, is avoiding me, but he really doesn't care all that much about me being back. If it were not for his father's return, I'm not sure if I would even be alive, baby or not. And Killian is just Killian, he always finds a way to be near me when he isn't busy.

"I'm so bored," Pixie whines. "It's not fair that I can't see my friends."

Turning the tap off, I let the bubbles cover my body as Pixie sits on the edge. "I know it sucks, but I made a lot of deals to find you. I can't go back on my word; they will kill me, and I just got you back. It's not safe right now. I will talk to Enzo about it when he gets back and see what I can do."

"You're the best," she says, leaning down to kiss my cheek. "I'm glad they found me."

"Same, I just wish I knew they found you, and I wouldn't have left."

Pixie sniffles. "Enzo would have made Kill hurt you, and he didn't want to do it. Sarge needs you, he won't say it, but he does, and Enzo is a big-headed dickhead."

I laugh. Pixie seems to have a dislike for Enzo, and it seems somewhat mutual in a playful way.

"I hate to say it, big sis, but I like it here, even if I am bored. I'm going to make us some dinner, the chef has been teaching me how to cook."

I nod. "I will find you when I have finished in here. And please don't burn the house down."

Pixie jumps up from the side of the tub and leaves the bathroom. Laying back, I relax and enjoy the warmth of the water until my fingers start to wrinkle. Getting out of the tub isn't easy, so I get out like an ungraceful baby elephant.

Once I'm dressed, I head downstairs and stop dead in my tracks. My mouth falls open. My eyes can't believe what they are seeing. A Viking of a man is using my sister to prop himself up.

"What did you do, Pix? They are going to kill you."

Both my sister and the bloody and battered man freeze.

"He didn't deserve to die, he saved me. He watched out for me after...after they hurt me."

"He is still a bad person, he sells people!" I yell, and Pixie scoffs as she struggles to hold up the man three times her size. I run my hands through my hair. This is bad, really fucking bad.

"And you don't think the dickhead you married hurts people? Or Kill? I know he does, I have watched him."

"Fuck, Pixie, you don't know what you have done. They will see this on the cameras." I wave my hands toward the security system Enzo has in place. Pixie follows with her eyes and shrugs.

"We can run, Lev will keep us safe."

I cackle and shake my head. "No, Pixie, he can't. You don't understand Killian's obsession with me, and I'm pregnant with Enzo's baby."

Think, Jordyn, think. Jumping from the steps, I move across the foyer. I have seen Sarge hide weapons everywhere. Finding a gun, I pull it out and turn, aiming at Lev.

"Let my sis..."

My words die off when I see he has a blade to her throat. "Don't make any sudden movements, I don't want to hurt her but I will. Put the gun down, she will call you and be returned as long as I walk out of here."

I nod. "Please don't hurt her, please," I beg, bending down slowly to place the gun on the floor.

Lev slowly walks across the foyer, toward the garage. Which seems weird that he knows where it is.

"I'm not a complete monster, I don't sell children. Expect a call in a few hours with a location."

"They are going to kill you," I tell him.

One of the security must have been notified. Three men run into the room; guns drawn. A scream peels from my lips, and I move in front of them. "Lower your fucking weapons."

"We can't do that," one of them says.

"If you don't, I will kill you all. My sister isn't getting hurt." None of the men lower their weapons. "I'm Mrs. Fucking D'Arco. Lower your motherfucking weapons now!"

One of them nods, and they all lower their guns. My heart pounds in my chest as Lev walks backward toward the garage.

"Hurt her, and I will hunt you down and become your worst nightmare."

Lev nods and disappears behind the door. I call down to the gate and demand they open them. I don't know what the hell my sister was thinking, but I need to call Enzo. It's better he hears it from me and not from one of his men.

CHAPTER SIX

KILLIAN

Being the enforcer for the D'Arco family should be very cut and dry. They bring me people, and I get them to talk. Except Enzo likes to take me on his little excursions, and I hate it. He is more than capable of dragging their asses back here.

Tonight, we had to have a meeting with Ivan; he doesn't know we have his son. The fucker insists he wasn't trading children, and normally I don't believe a word they say when they claim to be innocent, except Lev doesn't claim to be innocent. He sells women into the sex trade, that much he made clear. He says it's a punishment worse than death. What is wrong with all the crime families, so fucking soft they can't kill women?

Mario and Enzo have balls of steel, really coming into the Kozlov's estate while we have Ivan's son chained up in the basement. Of course, Ivan doesn't know that.

Once we get past security, they lead us up to Ivan's

office. Sarge takes note of how many men we pass, even if he is no longer head of security after he took his oath last night.

Ivan sits at his large desk, the bags under his eyes a dead giveaway the man is worried as fuck about his son.

"Mario," Ivan says in surprise.

"Ivan, it's good to see you. Though, after my visit today, I don't think you will feel the same way."

Ivan nods, and I trail my gaze to two of his biggest men that stand behind him. I eye them up and down, and if push comes to shove, I know I could take them. Sarge elbows me discreetly.

"How is it possible? I was at your funeral."

Mario exhales deeply. "I have vermin, and it seems your son was helping them."

Ivan's eyes go wide. "Even in my death, we had an understanding. No trafficking, and we would coexist in peace."

"And I honored our deal, I have no desire to sell children. I might be a monster..."

Mario laughs. "We are all monsters, but your son was involved in my disappearance. You know I can't let that slide."

"If you hurt my son," Ivan threatens, but Enzo finishes his sentence.

"We are going to war, we know. It's already done."

Ivan stands from his chair. "You killed my son!"

Now it's my turn to smirk. "Not yet, but it's a process I love to draw out."

He cuts an icy glare at me and starts spewing shit in Russian. I don't take my eyes off him, though. One word to his men and they could open fire, which I expected coming in. It's why my handy dandy killin' knife is in my boot.

Ivan's phone buzzes against the wooden desk. He looks down at it, and in frustration, he answers it. Enzo's phone does the same, but he lets it ring out.

A smirk raises on Ivan's face. Fuck, something is happening. When my phone vibrates in my pocket, I slide it out and see Jordyn's name light up the screen.

"Jordyn?"

Her cries fill me with dread. "He took her! I couldn't do anything."

I drop the phone onto the ground and slide the knife from my boot. Sarge watches me, and his jaw goes hard. Retrieving the phone, I put it back to my ear.

"Don't worry, Poppet, we will be back soon."

Ivan laughs. "It looks like my son is safe, after all."

I end the call, and before anyone can see it coming, Ivan has my best knife in the front of his neck; I love that first moment when their brain catches up. The room erupts in shouts, the two guards pull their weapons, Mario and Enzo dive for cover, and Sarge has already moved. Idiots think I only have one knife on me. They really should have patted me down better, but even the Russian guards have heard of me and my techniques and don't want to be put on my shit list.

Sarge ducks under the desk for cover but comes up with Ivan's gun and takes the first guy down while the second runs out into the hall and shouts in Russian. Footsteps get nearer, and I know we don't have a lot of time.

Enzo races to the dead guard and takes his gun. I run to Ivan and rip my blade from his throat.

"How the fuck are we getting out of this alive, Kill?" Enzo shouts, and I shrug.

"Knowing that your wife tried to call you and you didn't answer that...well, Lev has escaped and taken Pixie with him." I know this really doesn't answer his question, but I hope it gives him some motivation to make this exit snappy. We have a Russian to catch.

Sarge shakes his head and looks around the room. "Fuck, it looks like we need to run. I only counted six men here today, but that doesn't mean there are not more. I'll take the front and Kill, take the back."

Sarge pops his head out the door and quickly pulls it back in when a shot is fired. He composes himself and steps out, firing off a single shot. "Let's move. They will be waiting to ambush us downstairs."

We move out into the hall; Sarge extracts the weapon from the dead man's body and hands it to Mario.

As we slowly move down the stairs, a voice reaches us, "Come out, we have you surrounded."

I move past Mario and Enzo. "This is what is going to happen, I will run down and distract them, but you will all need to have my back."

"That's a fucking shit plan," Enzo snaps. "It's a sure way to die."

He isn't wrong, but I read once that if you run in a zigzag pattern, it's harder for them to hit you, so let's hope it holds some weight.

I shrug at Enzo, and he narrows his eyes at me with a glare as cold as ice. "Don't do it, that's an order."

I laugh at him; I haven't taken an oath, and I never will.

He knows that; I might kill for him, but I take orders from no man.

"Tell Poppet I love her," I say before running down the remaining stairs and out into the open foyer, where four men stand. They really were lacking manpower today. "Boo," I say, and they all point their guns at me. Just as the first guy fires, I drop to the ground and roll, bringing myself back up to my feet. Thankfully, the others have moved downstairs and are firing. I move my legs as fast as I can. Without a gun, I would need to get close enough to kill the man right up my ass. So, my plan is to make the asshole keep firing until he is out of bullets. Easier said than done.

Running in combat boots would be a hell of a lot easier if I tied the laces up, and one of the guards is hot on my heels as I race across the front lawn, so there's no time to tie them.

"Fucking shoot me," I yell, waiting for the bullet to come. Shit. One flies straight past my head, and I zag to the left. "Missed me."

Lucky for me, there are a heap of cars parked to the side of the house. I continue my zig-zag style of running with the guard hot on my heels.

I don't know what's happening inside the house, and I hope my distraction helped a little. The asshole following me doesn't even realize that I'm leading him to easier territory. Slipping in behind our SUV, I drop to the ground and search for his feet.

Where is the fucker? That's when I realize the mistake I have made and roll onto my back. The fucker is looking down on me from the top of the SUV, a shit-eating grin on his face, which is his first mistake. His cockiness leaves him open for me to inflict injury. I wait for him to blink, and the second his eyelids close, I flick the blade, and it hits him right in the dick. His gun fires, making my ears ring.

Someone shouts my name, and I roll to my side and see blood, lots of it. This isn't good. I should have aimed for his neck.

CHAPTER SEVEN

JORDYN

The minutes feel like hours, but only one question resonates in my mind. Why would Pixie do this? She said that she liked it here. She can't honestly be stupid enough to free a man from the basement and help him escape. How did she even get down there?

My call with Killian was disconnected, and I need them to come back so I can try to explain this shit show. Sitting on the stairs, I wait and wait.

"The property is clear," Kaser says, walking back into the room. He has at least six men in here. "We are doubling down on security; no one comes in or out."

One of the newer security guards comes and sits beside me. "Everything will be okay."

I nod, mainly because it's the automatic response that people want you to give them. Everything won't be okay, regardless of what he thinks. My sister somehow got into the basement, and I gave the order to open the fucking gate. I couldn't risk him hurting Pixie. He might have said he wouldn't, but men like that would sell their own grandmas to save their own asses.

"You did the right thing, красивый (beautiful)." My eyes widen, and I try to stand. "Alert them and your sister will go right back to where she came from. Do you understand me?" I nod. "I'm very disappointed in your men, leaving a beauty like you alone."

He runs a finger down my face. "Don't fucking touch me," I seethe between clenched teeth.

"I don't think that you are in any position to make demands. So listen well because this is what's going to happen. You won't say anything because if I don't call in within the hour, they will not return your sister."

When the front door is thrown open, I don't have a chance to respond. Sarge carries Killian in over his shoulder, his eyes connect with mine, and his brows furrow as he takes in the man next to me.

Sarge says something to Killian and Mario, and he points toward the basement. All the men move past us except Enzo; he comes toward me, and I hold my breath. I'm expecting him to rip me a new asshole over letting Lev out the gate.

I close my eyes momentarily, and when I open them, blood splashes against my face along with chunks of flesh.

Someone is screaming. I don't know who, but I think it could be me.

"Poppet... Damnit, put me down."

"You are losing too much fucking blood."

That was Sarge, I would recognize his voice anywhere.

"You take Jordyn upstairs; Enzo and I will take Kill to the basement."

Mario, I think, but I don't know. My whole body is trembling too hard to understand clearly.

"She is in shock, Sarge. Take her upstairs. I have enough training; I can sew that motherfucker up, and he will be ready to kick my ass for sticking him with a needle."

That voice isn't as recognizable. Kaser, I think. But I can't be sure.

Large arms carry me upstairs. I feel slightly detached from my body, and even though I keep willing myself to come back, it's like part of me doesn't want to.

Sarge sits me down on the toilet, and he runs the shower. He strips himself out of his clothes, and I stare aimlessly at him.

"We will need to dispose of our clothing. I'm going to undress you now, and we will wash the blood off."

Nodding, he helps me to my feet, and I do everything on autopilot: lifting my arms, stepping out of my underwear, stepping into the shower, and standing under the water, letting it wash away the man who had to call Lev so that my sister would be set free. I'm a terrible sister. How is it possible for her to be taken again?

I can't think about this, I need to focus and clear my head. I take a deep breath and look up at Sarge, who looks down at me with concern.

"Are you okay?"

When I shake my head no, I instantly break down. "I'm so sorry," I whisper. "I shouldn't have left you. Just know I didn't want to, please believe me."

He lets his forehead drop to mine and closes his eyes. "I wanted to run; I would have turned my back on my best friend."

"All I ever wanted to do was find my sister, and now I have fucked it all up again."

I drop to my knees slowly and blink up at Sarge, wrapping my hand around his cock, which hardens instantly. "You don't have to."

"I need to, or I will spiral straight back to where I was a few minutes ago. Bring me back, Sarge."

He nods, grips my hair hard, and thrusts into my open and willing mouth. It's funny how some things never change. I need to be strong and a man using me for their pleasure is where I have found my strength.

I flatten my tongue and hollow my cheeks, taking everything he is giving me. He is being too gentle. Pulling back, I run my tongue across the bead of pre-cum that forms on the tip, making his body shudder. I close my mouth back over his length, sucking him hard and deep. It's not long until his cum slides down the back of my throat. It's not enough to bring me back to where I need to be. Sarge is too nice to use me the way I need to be used right now.

He helps me out of the shower and into new clothes.

"You should rest," he says, pulling on a pair of sweats and a white muscle shirt.

"I will after I have seen Killian."

Sarge's shoulders slump; he knows that this is one battle he won't win. We walk in silence downstairs where men are cleaning chunks of the Russian's brain matter off the stairs.

"Clothes upstairs in the ensuite in the guest bedroom."

The man in a white hazmat suit nods at Sarge.

"Why did Enzo kill that man?"

"I told him to. The look in your eyes and the way you

were scared wasn't for Killian. It was already there. No one scares you, ever."

"He was Russian, he told me so."

Sarge nods but doesn't respond. My chest feels ready to cave in. I need Killian. The basement door is open, and Sarge follows in behind me. Killian is on a metal table, while Enzo and Mario watch as Kaser leans over his body.

"You have to let me touch you," Kaser demands.

"I'll fucking kill you!" Killian shouts. "I will rip your eyes out of your body."

"I'll do it," I say. "Killian can walk me through it, but everyone needs to get out."

"Doll, you don't call the shots here," Enzo says.

I take in a deep breath. "When it comes to him, I do. You have other shit to be doing like figuring out how a fucking Russian was posing as security, or how the fuck my sister had access down here because Lev took her, and if he doesn't hear from the man whose brain is splattered on the stairs, Lev won't let my sister go."

A large body steps up behind me. "I agree with her. If Killian won't let anyone touch him, then fuck the bastard. Let Jordyn have at him. We need to do our jobs now and keep everyone safe. Kill fucking killing Ivan complicates things. Lev won't let Pixie go straight away."

"I don't care what you do, but you need to fix it; you brought that man into this house, and he left with my flesh and blood."

Mario steps forward and places a hand on Enzo's shoulder. "You heard the woman; we have a job to do and my granddaughter to save. Pixie might not be my blood, but she is our family."

"Once I find her, she will be lucky if I don't fucking kill her myself," Enzo spits and goes off into a rampage in Italian. Kaser interrupts and points to Killian. Oh shit.

"Wear gloves and maybe chain him up so he doesn't accidentally kill you."

I snort. "I know how to handle him."

"The bullet is still inside him, you will need to dig it out with those," he says, pointing to a metal trolley with all kinds of grabby tools, and my stomach does back flips at the thought of digging them into his skin.

"If you need me, just yell out," Sarge says, still standing behind me.

Everyone clears out of the room, and I move toward Killian. He smiles up at me. "Hey, Poppet, ready to go fishing for a bullet?"

"You know that you're a pain in the ass, right?"

Pulling on a pair of gloves, I pick up some pointy looking pliers. These will have to do.

Looking back at Killian, he smiles. "What?"

"I think I might get shot more often."

I roll my eyes at him. Of course he would say something like that. "I will need to touch you so I can dig around. No killing me, please."

"I need you to handcuff me to the table, Poppet. If I black out, I have zero control."

He tells me where to find his handcuffs, and I don't even want to know why he has multiple pairs. Once he is secure, I take a deep breath and remove the gauze covering the wound and gag.

"Just dig in there."

I nod and do as he asks, but I can't feel anything with

these damn pliers. I lean over further and stick my finger in the hole, and the thing is definitely in there. Second time's a charm, the tip of the metal pliers hits the bullet. I carefully angle them so I can pull it out. I do it slowly, being careful not to hurt him. Kill has his eye on me the entire time.

"Stop watching me, you creeper."

He smiles, even though it doesn't reach his eyes. "No, I will be your creep because I'm committing this to memory. As soon as you have me fixed up, I'm going to fuck you."

I swallow hard. He means chain me up and fuck me, and fuck. A look I'm not familiar with crosses over Killian's face.

"Hey, Poppet, do me a favor and get that box on the top shelf down." Spinning, I look for what box he is talking about.

"How do you expect me to reach that?"

"There should be a stepladder over by the door."

I don't ask why he keeps it by the door. The man is crazy, and sometimes you just don't understand crazy. Once I have it set up, I get the box down, and it's full of metal letters.

"Find the J."

I gasp and look down at him. "Are you asking me to brand you, Killian?"

"I sure as fuck am. Gloves are on the counter, and the blowtorch is over by the basin."

I don't argue with him. That motherfucker branded me, so payback is a bitch. He walks me through setting it up, and I get to work. When the letter is glowing red, I put the torch down and raise my brow at him.

"Over the bullet hole, Poppet."

Nodding, I move closer and line the J up with the small hole and press it down against his skin. A roar of pain comes from him, and within seconds, Sarge is running down the stairs, taking in the scene in front of him.

"I don't even want to know," he says, shaking his head and leaving the same way he came in.

"So, we don't need to stitch it now?" I ask.

"No, Poppet, we don't. Now undo the cuffs so my cock can remember what it's like to be home again."

He doesn't need to ask me twice. The second his cuffs fall to the floor, he jumps from the metal table and has my arms behind my back.

"I won't hurt you this time. Enzo would kill me if I hurt his spawn, but I still plan to chain you up. Hands in the air."

My hands raise on their own accord, and Killian chains me to the ceiling, just like last time, except my feet can touch the ground this time around. He pulls out his favorite knife as he circles me, running the blade along my collarbone.

"I can't wait until the day I can see your blood run for me again."

I buck my body a little, causing the blade to lightly slice my skin. "Tut, tut, are you trying to get me killed?"

I moan, "I'm trying to get you to fuck me, Killian. I need your cock inside me."

With a flick of his wrist, my shirt is sliced down between my breasts. He drops the knife and uses his hands to rip the shirt from my body.

Stepping back, he runs his eyes over me, from my head to my toes. "Holy fuck, you're a sight."

His words spark something inside me I haven't felt since before I was pregnant. I'm at the point in my pregnancy where I feel fat and gross. I don't have a perfect little bump like the images I see on the pregnancy pamphlets.

He bends down in front of me and slides my yoga pants down my legs, taking my underwear with them.

"We are going all natural, I like it."

"If I can't see it, I'm not shaving it," I state matter-of-factly, and I stand by it. I can no longer bend myself like a damn fucking pretzel.

Killian doesn't seem bothered; his head moves between my legs, and his tongue breaches my lips, opening me up. His hands slide to my ass, and his fingers dig into the skin, pulling me into his face as his tongue pushes inside me while his nose moves across my clit. When I feel the inkling of an orgasm, he pulls back.

I whine in hopes he'll resume, but he stands, causing me to pout. I need a release so badly. He walks behind me, and I twist my body so I can see what he is up to. He goes straight for the freezer and pulls out his fucking ice dildo.

Coming back to me, the ice is cold against my neck, and he slowly moves it across my neck. Small droplets of water melt and run down my sternum, and his tongue catches them, sending goosebumps over my body. The ice moves down and circles my nipple, which hardens in pleasure from the assault of the cold.

I pant like a bitch in heat the lower the ice gets. My moans of pleasure fill the room, a vast difference from the sounds this space normally hears. He reaches my clit, and my eyes roll back into my head.

"Killian, fuck me, please. I can't take it anymore. I need you."

The ice slides through my lips, and as he circles my needy hole, she tries to suck in the ice, needing whatever Killian is willing to give. He leans in and sucks my nipple into his mouth, lightly biting down. I know he is holding back, and I wish he could be rough, but I'm thankful for his self-control.

"Once this baby is out of you, I want to fuck you bloody and bruised with the ice in your ass while your tight little cunt strangles my cock."

"Please," I beg; I want that so badly.

He slowly inserts the ice dildo inside me, and my pussy clamps around it, needing more. Pulling it out, he brings it to my lips, and I open for him, sucking my juices off the ice. When he is happy that I have sucked every single inch of the ice, he removes it from my mouth and drops it to the ground. The ice shatters at our feet.

Killian undoes his belt, and his jeans drop to his feet, his massive cock erect and ready. He wraps his hand around his length and strokes himself, his thumb running over the tip, swiping off some pre-cum. He drops his cock and brings his thumb to my lips, and smears it across my mouth. My tongue darts out and glides across the salty wetness as he lifts me by my hips.

He hesitates for a moment; Killian's cock is big, so big that without the right prep, he could rip you in half.

"Fuck me, Killian, I can take it. I'm not as fragile as you think I am."

His eye goes dark. "You think you can take all of this?"

I nod and whimper as he lines himself up and thrusts deep. A shrill scream escapes me, and footsteps can be heard, but Killian doesn't let up. My eyes close, and I lean my head back as his thrusts become harder, my tits bouncing with each movement.

"I'm going to fuck this pussy for the rest of my life. Do

you know how dangerous that is, Poppet, a man like me owning you?"

"Oh fuck, Killian... I have heard those words before, and you didn't come for me."

"I knew where you were, and it was only a matter of time before I came, but mark my words, if you ever leave me, I will hunt you to the end of the earth and leave a wake of bodies behind. And when I find you, I won't give you what you want, I will edge you until just seeing me is painful. You will beg me to take pity on you."

An orgasm wrecks my entire body, I can feel it in the tip of my toes as it explodes. "Killian!!!"

He must come at the same time as he roars in satisfaction at the same time I scream his name. All I want is to sag against his body, but that isn't who he is. A throat clears behind us, and Enzo leans against the door frame and pushes off, stalking toward us. Killian unhooks me before he even tucks his cock away. Enzo scoops my limp body into his arms and heads upstairs.

"I'm naked," I protest, and Enzo just laughs.

"No one would be stupid enough to look at what belongs to me."

My eyes close at his reassurance knowing him, Sarge, and Killian will be the only ones to lay their eyes on me in this state, and honestly, I'm so sated right now, I could sleep for an entire week.

CHAPTER EIGHT

ENZO

Jordyn fell asleep after I carried her upstairs. I wanted nothing more than to spread her legs and tongue fuck the shit out of her while she had Killian's cum dripping from her cunt, but I didn't because while I'm still pissed off about my mom, I know that neither my father nor I could have ended her. She did my father a huge favor by doing it.

Kaser comes running into the foyer. "Boss, you're needed in your office."

He turns and I follow him back. My father has the phone to his ear the moment I enter the door. I wanted to get rid of the house line, it's so fucking outdated, but Aldo had said my father kept it for this exact reason, so your enemies can easily get in contact but don't have your personal number.

My father puts the call on speakerphone. "Where is Pixie?" I growl.

"Agh, Enzo, how nice of you to join us. I'm normally a man of my word but imagine my surprise when I got home and found my father was murdered."

"You brought this war to your own front door," I snap. Sarge puts his hand on my shoulder, and I relax enough that I don't get the girl killed by the end of the call.

"I'm a man of my word, no harm will come to the girl, but I need her as an insurance policy. Listen and listen well, мой друг (my friend.)"

"I'm not your friend."

Lev laughs. "Maybe we should have been friends," he says in such a condescending tone, I just know there's a smirk on his face. "I had no involvement in your family trying to kill your father or selling children. Your mother came to me with a deal I couldn't refuse. I don't take pleasure in physically hurting women, so I sold them to her. They were evil women who deserved what they got. Certainly not innocent."

"Let me talk to Pixie, so I know she is alive."

Again, Lev laughs. "Enzo, this is not a hostage situation, маленькая бабочка (little butterfly) is not scared of me, she is my friend."

That makes me laugh. "She is a child, you fucking prick."

"Calm your tits, dickhead. I'm fine. I will be back before you can even miss me," Pixie says.

Rage builds deep inside over the whole damn situation. Jordyn needs to explain what the fuck is going on and what happened. My father insisted I didn't push her, but it's obvious the old fool has gone fucking soft in the time he has been away.

"I'm going to fucking kill you when you get back," I seethe.

My father clears his throat. "What he means to say is we miss you and be safe."

"If you want her to be safe, you will step back and leave me alone to create my empire, the same way my father did for Enzo. You have my word that I will sell no children, but the women are fair game. None are innocent, and as for my father's death, I'm taking back the territory you acquired of ours. I should thank you, Killian."

Kill just walked through the door, cleanly showered, and his brows dip. "What's the Russian Viking-looking motherfucker thanking me for?"

"Killing my father. Nice aim, by the way. I would have had to outsource, so my family followed me, but now, you created monsters who will eat out of the palm of my hand."

"When do we get the girl back?" Kill asks, not responding to his gloating about his father's death.

"Maybe a day, a week, or a year. It depends on if I sense any push back."

"I will just kill you fucking both," I seethe.

"Bring it, dickhead, and I will tell my sister you planned to kill me all along," Pixie declares. Damn kid is a firecracker.

They end the call, and I look around the room, finding everyone waiting for me to explode. I knock the fucking phone from the desk and storm from the room. Jordyn needs to get up and walk me through what the fuck her sister's deal is.

I end up taking the stairs two at a time until I reach the top and enter Jordyn's room. Even though I have forced her to sleep in mine, I let her rest in here. She is curled up in a ball with her hand cradling her stomach. All the pent-up rage that was bubbling over starts to fizzle out, and I imagine what my son will look like. Will he get her cute little button nose, or will he get mine that's been passed down for generations? She stirs and must feel my presence.

She blinks her eyes open and looks around the room. "What's wrong?" she asks, sitting up as fast as someone who is pregnant can.

"Lev called."

Her eyes widen, laced with fear. "Is Pixie okay?"

I nod. "She is, but I need you to explain what happened."

"Only if you promise not to kill my sister."

Sighing, I run my hand through my hair. "I don't kill children, Doll. I might strangle her for calling me a dickhead; even when she has been kidnapped, she still pushes my fucking buttons."

Jordyn chuckles, and I hadn't realized until now that I like when she is happy. "She was cooking us dinner while I took a bath. When I came downstairs, she was helping Lev. I tried to get one of Sarge's guns, but he had one of Killian's knives to her throat."

I already know most of this, the cameras picked up what happened, but I need her to recount the details I couldn't see.

"He promised he would let her go once he was out, so I forced your security to lower their weapons and open the gate. I couldn't risk her being hurt."

"Why did she help him?"

Jordyn looks up at me, her big blue eyes filled with tears. "She said he helped her when the men hurt her. She said he didn't deserve to die. I tried to reason with her that he was a dangerous man, but she had a good point when she said you were also not a good man."

I shrug. She isn't wrong, and I get it, Pixie isn't loyal to my family. She is loyal to her sister, but it also seems that Lev is now someone she is loyal to.

"Is he letting her go?"

"I don't know. He says that he will, but when is another question. We need to think smart because if we extract her, and she doesn't want us to... I can't have another rat under my roof, so if she comes back, her loyalty needs to be with us. I'll have my men find their location so we can keep tabs on them. If at any time she looks like she is in trouble, we will forcefully remove her, but until then..."

Jordyn rolls out of bed. "Are you fucking kidding me? You need to bring her back, she is just a child." She walks into the closet, and I follow behind her as she throws on an oversized shirt that belongs to Sarge and a pair of leggings.

"A child who made an adult fucking decision to help a prisoner in my house escape. If that were anyone else, they would be fucking dead. Do you understand this is not shit we fuck around with?"

"Then we will leave," she snaps, trying to push past me. I grab her arm and pull her into my body.

"You don't want to fuck around and find out what happens if you leave again. When Kill hunts you down, I won't let my best friend's feelings for you get in the way. You might have earned yourself immunity, but maybe I will make a deal with my enemy and sell you to him. Wouldn't that be fun?"

"Do it," she sneers, "You might have Sarge's undying loyalty now that he has taken his oath, but you don't have Killian's, and you never will. He is a lone wolf who doesn't want a fucking pack. I will fuck my way through all the men and send him videos. How long will it be until he can't take it anymore and burns the world to the ground and everyone in it? I would relish in a death by his hands."

My hand strikes out, and my fingers wrap around her throat. She knows she has hit a nerve, and she smirks at me and arches her neck, taunting me.

"If you wanted an obedient wife, you should have married Cat. I may have been waiting it out until my sister was found, but I'm from Huntersville and have had to fight my entire fucking life to survive. I'm the fucking queen of this empire now, so you should be on your knees worshiping me."

Before I can even respond, the air is sucked from my lungs and pain radiates up into my stomach, and I drop to the ground and cradle my nuts. Doll looks down over her stomach and laughs at me. "And that was for letting that woman around my sister. She is a fucking snake. You could have called Harper...oh my fuck, I haven't even called my best friend!"

She rushes around the room while I lay on the ground, holding my nuts. Killian walks into the room; I know it's him by the combat boots that stop beside my head.

"She kicked you in the balls."

I nod, and he offers me his hand so that I can sit up.

"I will see you soon," Doll says and turns back to glare at me. "Harper is on her way. Make sure she is on the list or so help me, I will start shooting your fucking staff."

She storms toward the door, and when she turns back abruptly, she looks straight at Killian. "When you know my sister's location, I want to be the first person you tell."

Kill nods. "Yes, Ma'am."

She turns and storms straight from the room. "You're fucking pussy whipped."

A deep-rooted laugh comes from him. "Don't even pretend that you're not. We both know she should have been killed so many times by now. You can use Sarge as your excuse all you like."

"Fuck you," I say jokingly. He backhands me in the stomach.

"Nah, bro, I will leave that for Sarge."

The asshole leaves the room, and I follow behind.

CHAPTER NINE

JORDYN

Enzo finally made an appointment with an obstetrician that is a friend of the family. We sit in the waiting room, along with Mario and Kaser, while I fill out the paperwork. When I ask Enzo about insurance, he just says that he will pay cash today and get it sorted out later.

A beautiful woman exits a room, and Mario jumps to his feet and meets her halfway, where he pulls her into his arms.

Enzo stands and offers me his hand, pulling me to my feet, and takes the paperwork. "Enzo," the woman says in a slightly clipped tone, which tells me that the motherfucker has fucked her. Jealousy works its way into my stomach, which surprises me. I shake it off when she turns to me.

"And you must be Jordyn, it's nice to meet you."

"You too," I say politely, even though I'm not sure I actually mean it.

She leads us into her office and hands me a small container and asks me to go pee in it before we start. I do as she asks and leave her office, Kaser hot on my heels. He opens the door to the single stall bathroom and makes sure it's empty.

Once he leaves, I close the door and quickly pee in the little container, and when I'm finished, Kaser is still waiting for me.

He follows me back to the room, but he doesn't come inside; he closes the door and stays outside.

"Thank you. I should have introduced myself first, I'm Lucia Mancini."

I blink at her. "As in Catalina's relative."

I turn to Enzo. "Are you serious right now? You fucked her, and yet you have an issue with Angelo screwing Catalina...Ugh, I don't even care."

Lucia chuckles. "Cat is my sister, and I can assure you that we are nothing alike, and as for the sex, it was once and revenge sex. Catalina also had relations with my ex-fiancé."

"I should knee you in the dick again."

Mario bellows out a laugh. "Can we get to the part where I can see my grandchild? I'm an old man and only aging faster."

Lucia laughs. "Mario, you are fifty, that is barely ancient. But yes, let's get you up on the table. From your notes, I see that you're twenty-eight weeks, going by your last menstrual cycle."

"Yes, I was on the pill, and when I got sick, I forgot to take the pill for however long Killian had me knocked out."

"Taking the pill during early pregnancy is not the end of the world. I'm sure everything will be fine. Did you have any prenatal care?"

"A private midwife came to see me a handful of times. Being on the run didn't really allow for much else."

"So, you haven't seen this little guy yet?"

I shake my head no. "No, DNA was done by blood test, and they asked if I wanted to know the sex."

Lucia nods, and Enzo helps me up onto the table. I lay back and pull up my shirt, then Lucia shakes a bottle and squirts it onto my stomach.

Lucia turns the screen, and tears well in my eyes at the sight on the screen. My son's face stares back at me.

"He has lots of hair," she says.

"How can you tell? It looks like a skull to me," Enzo says, and Lucia points out the hair, and she snaps pictures. She takes all of his measurements, and we get pictures of his little feet and hands.

Enzo holds my hand the entire time, and when I gaze up at him, his eyes water.

"He looks absolutely healthy; his estimated weight is just a little over two pounds, and he is fourteen inches long. Have you picked a name yet?"

Enzo shakes his head no. "Actually, I was thinking we would stick to tradition and call him Mario, but Mars for short."

Mario starts talking in Italian. I have no idea what he is saying, but it must be good. The man cries tears of happiness and pulls Enzo into his arms. Lucia laughs. "You have made him a very happy man, and Mars is a very nice name."

"It's perfect," Enzo says, leaning down to press a kiss to my lips. He freezes momentarily, clearly caught up in the moment.

"Thank you for giving me this gift," Mario says.

Lucia excuses herself to get the images ready to email to

us. "I'm going to be a father," Enzo says to no one in particular.

Once Lucia comes back with a printed image, she says that she has forwarded the images to my email. I can't wait to show the others, and Harper is meeting me at the house. The one person that I wish I could talk to isn't here, and the happiness I felt a moment ago dissipates until all I'm left with is a pang of guilt.

Enzo drives us home when the appointment is done, and when we get there, Harper's car is in the driveway. Killian and Sarge drive in behind us, then Sarge steps out and pulls his sunglasses off his face and sits them on top of his head. We haven't officially cleared the air, but he seems a lot less tense around me, and when he smiles, I take that as a sign to approach.

"How did it go?" he asks as we walk side by side toward the house.

"Good. Lucia printed me a picture, do you want to see?"

Sarge nods, and I hand him the small, printed image. "I can't wait to meet him."

Mario comes up beside us. "Did she tell you the good news?" Sarge looks at me, and I shrug. "That they are naming the baby Mario."

"Mars for short," I say. "Mars Andrew Masters D'Arco."

Sarge's eyes go wide. "Andrew, as in…"

"Your middle name, yes. I might have snooped and looked at your license."

Killian comes up behind me. "I'm honored, Poppet."

"I don't know your middle name, so I couldn't work with that."

He quickly laughs behind me. "I don't have a middle name."

I abruptly stop in the foyer, and Killian bumps into me. I turn to face him. "Who doesn't have a middle name, that's so weird."

Killian shrugs. "I'm surprised anyone cared enough to give me a first name."

A squeal comes from in the sitting room, and Harper comes bouncing out. "Where are the pictures? Aunty Harper is dying over here. First, I find out that you're back and pregnant on the same day; I need more after missing out on months of your life. You promised me online baby shopping." She turns to Enzo. "Hand over the credit card, buddy. Babies need things, and this one is getting the best. You can afford it."

Enzo reaches for his wallet and pulls out a black card and hands it to Harper. "If you need any help, call Mercedes, I'm sure she would love to help. If you leave the house, you are to take a security team with you and are to notify me."

"Yes, Boss," Harper says, saluting him.

"I have contractors coming in this week. They will redo the west wing. Our set up isn't ideal at the moment, and when Pixie is back, she can take your room, so it will be her wing once we remodel. The decorator will be here next week for you to give her your input."

"Why are you redoing the house? The baby would sleep with me."

"Angelo's wing is bigger; it was designed for us as kids. I took my father's wing. We are all in this together, Doll. We need a space for us all and one for the baby and one for the night nurse."

"Night nurse?"

Harper grabs me by the arm. "Let's go spend his money, and you can argue about a night nurse after you push the baby out of your coochie. You could change your mind yet."

"Fine," I huff.

"Let's go and find the most expensive things that we can."

Enzo laughs as Harper drags me into the kitchen. Sarge comes in on our heels and hands us a laptop and kisses me on the cheek, then leaves us be.

Killian comes in next. "Poppet, come find me later, yeah?"

He moves around the kitchen and into the pantry, bringing out a box of lucky charms, and places them down in front of me. He knows I have a weakness for dry cereal. I smile up at him, and he places a kiss on my head and leaves the kitchen.

Harper has the laptop open and is scouring baby sites. She gets up and raids the cupboards until she finds a pen and paper, and we start a list of big items that we will need.

Harper talks a million miles a minute, and when she does, it's normally because she has something that she wants to tell me but wants me to pry.

"Out with it."

She looks up from the notepad. "What?"

I roll my eyes at her. "Harp."

She sighs and then smiles. "So, I have this client who comes in, and I got my pretty woman moment." What is with her and wanting a pretty woman moment? "It's not as good as yours, but we went to a gala, and it wasn't just him." She lowers her voice, as if anyone here cares. "Three, and now I know what it's like to be you. Even if it was just one night."

"So, what's the problem?"

Harper shrugs. "He hasn't come back since. He normally comes to see me twice a week, and it's been over a week."

"Do you know anything about him?"

She shrugs. "His name is Van, or Sullivan."

Someone chokes on a half cough, and both Harper and I turn to see Angelo in the doorway. I scowl at him.

"What do you want?" I snap.

He uses us knowing he is there as an excuse to move into the kitchen.

"I know I'm not your favorite person in the world, but you're not talking about Sullivan O'Brien, are you? Because I hate to break it to you, but if there were a thing between you two," he says, pointing at Harper, "your friendship would be over. We don't fuck with the Irish."

Harper rolls her eyes; she doesn't get how serious it really is. Wars break out between families.

"Look, Angelo, they pay to fuck me. I'm a whore. If you paid me, I would fuck you as well. It's my job. So why don't you focus on whatever it is that you do."

Angelo shrugs. "Jordyn, I want to apologize for my behavior. I just thought you were some random chick my brother brought home to piss off our mother."

"Let's just start fresh, but if you so much as even make a sexual move toward me, I will tell Killian and let you have a turn in the basement while I watch."

Angelo nods. "Noted, and watch your back when it comes to Cat. She has had her claws in my brother for so long that I only fucked her in hopes he would kick her to the curb. But she is like that sex tape you made in college that keeps resurfacing."

I snort. "Can't say I have made one or even went to college."

"Shame, that's a video I would watch."

Harper laughs, but I raise my brow at him and open my mouth, "Kil...."

Angelo raises his hands and backs away with a shit-eating grin on his face. He might not be my favorite person in the world, but he is Enzo's underboss, which means he isn't going anywhere anytime soon.

CHAPTER TEN

JORDYN

Harper finally leaves after we spend a small fortune on baby supplies. I have no idea what a diaper genie is, but I now have one being delivered. The breast pump looks like a small torture device that Killian would have in the basement. Speaking of Killian, he asked me to find him after Harper left. Pushing the door open to the basement, I freeze when I hear his voice.

"I already told you I don't give a fuck. You're not my family because my family wouldn't have sent me away to be fucking tortured day in and day out for most of my childhood. If any of you come near me or mine, I will fillet you like a fucking fish and make you the next meal at family dinner."

I take a deep breath and make myself known. Killian looks up at me as I enter and points to the chair that is situated next to a small desk in the corner.

"My loyalty," he scoffs. "None of you would know the

first thing about fucking loyalty. How is this for loyal? When I see you next, I will fucking end you."

Killian launches his phone at the wall, and it shatters, parts of the device flying around the door. I don't bother sitting; I close the distance between us.

"Poppet," he warns.

"Don't try to use your scary voice on me. What's going on?"

He leans his forehead down and presses it against mine. "Just someone who claims to be family, but mine died twenty-nine years ago. Those who knew I existed abandoned me. I'm not about to make nice now. You're my family, and Enzo and Sarge."

"Why don't you take the oath then, be part of Enzo's family?"

Killian pulls back and looks down at me. He may not like the way he looks, but he is handsome as fuck, even with the acid burns.

"I just can't," he whispers. "That would make it real."

I nod because I understand what he means. Being here can be hard, and seeing Enzo with his family, even if they are dysfunctional, they are powerful, and they love each other. Maybe minus their mother because she was the worst of the worst. A mother who sells children into a sex ring is a disgrace to women.

"What did you want to talk to me about?" Killian takes my hand and leads me to the desk where he asked me to sit. He flicks on the screen, and I can see surveillance of someone's house. "I don't understand."

"Flick through," he says, leaning over the back of the chair, his head resting on my shoulder.

I gasp. "It's Pixie."

"It is. I wanted you to know that I'm tracking her. Lev will be waiting for us to retaliate, and this time we are being smart. She isn't in any immediate danger. She has been following Lev around the house, and he smiles at her. He shot one of his men because it looked like they got into an argument over her."

"Isn't that weird? He is ten years older than her, at least."

Killian chuckles. "If he was interested in her sexually, yes, but it seems he has been nothing but respectful. And Poppet, you do know I'm thirteen years older than you."

"That's different. I'm a consenting adult, and Killian Masters, you are hot as fuck. I have no self-control around you."

"I have the most self-control around you; if I didn't, you would be dead."

I laugh "Why do you make my death at your hands sound so appealing?"

Flicking through the screens, I watch my sister make something to eat in Lev's kitchen, shaking her ass as she bounces around. She looks happy.

"Let me go!" someone snaps. Both Killian and I turn to see two of Enzo's cousins come through the door, with a young man trapped between them.

"I just have to deal with this," Killian says and places a kiss on my cheek.

The man behind me squeals, but I don't bother turning to see what's happening because I have a good idea already. He will know what it means facing Kill, and it really sucks to be him right now.

"I will have Enzo's money soon, I promise."

One of the other men who brought him in, laughs. "That's what you have been saying for weeks."

Oomph. That didn't sound nice. I twirl my chair around and find the two men are holding the man up while Killian chains him to the beam on the ceiling.

"Are we really doing this with her in the room?"

I smile at the man. "I would be really careful what you say next," I add, and the man sneers at me.

"*We* are not doing anything with Enzo's wife in the room. *I* am, so be good little boys and run along."

One man remains silent—smart man—but the other's mouth opens, and Killian steps forward, his blade in his hand, and he holds it close to the man's stomach.

"Don't even try to question me. If you have an issue, go take it up with your cousin, Luca. No one watches me work."

Luca's eyes cut to mine, as if to say why is she here, then he looks back at Killian and nods.

"Call us when you need us to pick him up," the other man says.

It's so bad that I don't know all of Enzo's cousins' names, but he has so many, and I'm not even sure if they are all even actually related or not.

Killian steps back, and both men leave. He winks at me before he turns his attention to the man hanging from chains.

"Milo, how many times do I have to see you down here? I really don't want to have to kill you, kid."

Milo shrugs. "I feel honored, and I promise I don't enjoy our time together."

The idiot smiles at Killian, who just shakes his head. The door to the basement opens, and Sarge walks in.

"Hey Milo, did you miss us that much?" Sarge jokes.

"Nah, I wouldn't miss your ugly faces. I heard the boss man got married, and I thought I would come and meet his wife."

Sarge laughs and holds out his hand and pulls me to my feet. He takes my spot and pulls me back down on his lap, wrapping his arms around my stomach.

"What are you doing down here?" Sarge whispers in my ear.

"Just watching my sister. The little shit is living her best life. I want to storm in there and shake the shit out of her."

"Want to take your frustrations out on Milo?" Killian asks, and I bite my lip and nod. Sarge helps me up from his lap, and I walk over to where Milo stands.

"Hi, I'm Milo, nice to meet you. I would shake your hand but..." He looks up at his hands and tries to wiggle them.

"Jordyn, I hope you don't mind me practicing on you."

Milo smiles at me, and Killian hands me a bat. My eyes go wide. Maybe I am not so cut out for this.

"You try to use your legs to hurt her, and I will cut them off and beat you with them," Killian says, and Milo nods.

Killian helps me understand where to hold my hands on the bat, and we practice swinging. I press my back against his front, relishing in the contact between us. It's very limited that he will naturally touch anyone without freezing up.

"Ready?" he asks, and I nod.

He helps me pull the bat back far enough and just as we are about to swing... "Wait!"

"Poppet, we need to hurt him, even just a little, so he learns his lesson."

I snort. "I don't think he is learning if he keeps coming

back, but if he owes you money, how does he make his money?"

"I play Blackjack," Milo says.

"So, he needs hands, let's take out his legs, he can use a wheelchair for a few weeks."

"I like the way you think," Milo says with a wink. Killian forces my arms to move, and the bat connects with Milo's leg. He screams out in pain.

"Don't ever wink at my woman," Killian snarls.

Milo looks between Killian and me. "Are you in one of those poly relationships? I would be down to find one. How much easier is it and is group sex a thing..."

Milo screams out again when I swing the bat, and it connects with the same leg. "Don't ever ask me about my sex life," I snap. I don't mind sharing with Harper because she is my best friend.

"Fuck, you make me hard," Killian whispers in my ear. "Again, on the other side."

Killian pulls the bat back, and I swing again. Milo screams out.

"I think we are good now, but if I see you again down here, Milo, I will cut my losses and kill you."

He moans in pain. "Sure thing, I will miss our time together."

I snort. Something is wrong with this kid. I know I should feel bad for him, but I'm learning that if you mess with the Mafia, then you're well aware of the consequences if you fuck up. Men normally come here to die, so I wonder why this kid was brought here instead of Enzo's cousins roughing him up.

Killian helps him down and sits him on a seat. "I'll call your father to come get you."

Milo complains, "Why would you call him? He wants me to live a hippy life like him, and I like Wi-Fi."

"Cal is my brother."

Hairs prickle on the back of my neck. I don't know a whole lot about Killian's family.

Milo scoffs. "Barely, you grew up together."

Killian leans down and gets in his face. "We were tortured together, we survived together. He is my brother in every sense of the word, besides blood."

"Jesus fuck, Killian," I snap. "You made me hurt your nephew? What is wrong with your head?"

Killian laughs. "Poppet, you don't want to know the answer to that."

"If you just let me work for you, I wouldn't need to gamble."

"No," Killian snaps, and I keep looking between them both. Sarge still sits quietly in the office chair, but he has his back to us and is clicking through the surveillance footage.

"Why not?" I ask Killian. "You could teach him everything you know, and that way when you retire, you have someone to take your place."

Killian raises a brow at me and then looks at Milo. "Could you even kill a man and feel nothing? And what if the cops, or worse, another family, kidnaps and tortures you? Would you talk?"

Milo shrugs. "I killed a cow once and felt really bad, but the guys that come in here, I suspect, deserve to die."

"I'm a bad fucking man. If you screwed up, I would be responsible, and your father would kill me himself."

"Come on, Uncle Kill, give me a chance. Let me go through the process of what your soldiers go through, and if I can survive that, you can give me a shot because we both know once you let me leave, I will fuck up again, and then you will be forced to kill me anyway."

Killian looks at me again, and I shrug. "Fine," he says through gritted teeth, "but if he screws up, you get to explain it to his father and Enzo."

I nod. "Deal, because if anyone tries to hurt me, I have you to protect me." Killian smiles at me. It's not often that he gives those out, but when he does, it melts my fucking heart, and I love it.

"And me," Sarge says with conviction as I glance over at him and wink. There was never a doubt in my mind that he had my back.

"And we need to get in touch with Lev. Your sister likes him too much, and I think we can use that to get her back. I will get Enzo to send him a message and organize a meeting."

"Sarge, can you take Milo upstairs to my room, and Killian, you call a doctor? Let's get him fixed up, and once he is healed, he can start his initiation, or whatever the fuck you call it."

Both men stare at me and nod. Milo laughs. "Man, you two are pussy whipped. I can't wait to see how bad Enzo is. I think we will be great friends."

Sarge picks Milo up with ease; he winces but gives me a wave. Killian watches them leave and shakes his head. "I'm going to regret this."

"Maybe, maybe not. Keeps the kid out of trouble, and you seem to have a soft spot for him."

Killian growls. "The only person I have a soft spot for is you."

"Good, because I might need your protection from Enzo when he finds out I'm responsible for you bringing Milo in without asking him first."

I doubt he will care that much; he wants what's best for his friends, and it's good for Killian to not isolate himself down here all the time.

CHAPTER ELEVEN

SARGE

Staying mad at Jordyn is impossible, she isn't Missy, and I can't keep projecting my feelings onto her. That and when she is curled up in my bed, my arm slung over her waist and the baby kicking, I feel complete.

I tuck a strand of hair behind her ear as she sleeps. She looks peaceful, even though I know as soon as she wakes up, she will be haunted by her past, just like I am.

Enzo organized a meet with Lev today on neutral ground. A bar the Python's leader Venom's woman owns. It became a place where we could meet and do business, where no weapons are allowed. If you wanna fight there, you need to use your fists, and then risk Venom blowing your brains out if you piss off his woman.

Jordyn rolls onto her back, and the first thing I notice is that her stomach has grown immensely over the last week. Leaning over, I place a kiss on her stomach. "Hey, buddy," I say in a low voice. "You're going to be one spoiled baby, you know that? I'm going to teach you how a man should love a woman, and Kill will probably teach you everything your momma won't want him to, and your dad, well, he will show you how to be a true leader, so that one day you will be able to take over for him and lead the family."

"If you don't stop talking to him, he will keep kicking my bladder, and I might piss my pants."

"Hmm, water sports. I'm not opposed to it."

She whacks me on the arm, and I laugh at her. I'm not yucking anyone's kink, but she can keep her pee to herself.

"Why don't you go pee, and then I can give you a proper good morning wake up?"

Her eyes pop open, and she searches my face before she smiles. "That sounds like a good plan, will you include breakfast?"

When I nod, she rolls out of bed awkwardly and waddles her sexy ass to the ensuite. Wasting no time, I slide my briefs down my legs and kick them onto the floor.

When she steps back out of the ensuite, a smile creeps up onto her face, and she lifts her nightshirt over her head. Fuck, her tits are beautiful, so big and round and full. Next, she shimmies her underwear over her hips, lets them drop to the floor, and steps out of them.

My eyes travel down her body, and I notice that she has shaved. It didn't bother me that she wasn't; I wouldn't either if I couldn't see my cock anymore.

"Killian took pity on me and shaved the bush off with his favorite blade. It better look good because it was the scariest time of my fucking life."

I bellow out a laugh because, of course, Kill couldn't be normal and use a razor on the poor woman. Instead, he took a fucking blade to the one part of her body we all couldn't live without. Her cum is so sweet, I wish I could bottle it up and savor it.

I motion for her to move closer, which she does, and once she gets to the edge of the bed, she crawls up and straddles my waist.

She doesn't get nervous or wait for instruction anymore; she grips my cock and pumps it a few times, then lines it up with her wet hole and sinks down. My eyes roll into the back of my head. There is nothing better than that first moment your brain registers the feeling of being buried inside a pussy.

She places her hands on my chest and runs her finger over Missy's name. "Can we go and visit her together? I would like to talk to her." Tears well in my eyes, and I nod my head. "Thank you."

Gripping her hips, I guide her to move before I bust my nut while we talk about my wife. "You don't have to thank me, now ride my cock so I can blow inside you and text a picture of it to your husband, and we can place bets on how fast he finds you."

"Yes please," she says, bucking her hips. Her and Enzo are still on rocky ground, but the one thing neither can deny is the sexual attraction. Enzo needs to realize Jordyn didn't want to hurt his mother, and if she didn't take her life, shit would be a complete mess with Mario back. Family members would have had to vote on what to do with her since she had immunity being the mother of the Don's children. Her crimes started when Mario was head of the family, hence why it would come down to a vote. People would have been put in a really shit position. And Jordyn needs to realize that everything Enzo does is for the family, which now includes her. He won't do anything to ever put her in danger.

Once she gets into a steady rhythm, my hands glide over her body, over the roundness of her hips, and the curve of her waist—even though it's not as prominent anymore, it's still there—and up to cup her breasts. Her head falls back when I roll her nipples between my fingers.

Her soft moans make me need to taste her lips. Letting go of her nipples, I lean forward and capture her mouth. Her tongue automatically seeks out mine and muffles the sounds she makes. Her whole body spasms around me, the tight warmth of her orgasm sending me over the edge.

She lifts herself off me and flops down next to me. I grab my phone off the nightstand and move down the bed, spreading her legs. I set the phone to video mode and swipe my fingers through my cum, pushing it back inside her.

She chuckles when I move back up beside her. "How long?" she asks.

"Five minutes, he is in a zoom meeting right now," I say as I hit send. I laugh as I also forward it to Killian. Let's see which one can run faster. I doubt Kill is even awake yet. He was up late, and there was a lot of yelling coming from the basement. Cal was told about Milo becoming Kill's new protégé, and he didn't take the news well.

"I give him two."

Setting the stopwatch on my phone, we wait. One minute and thirty-three seconds later the door is kicked open, and Enzo stands at the entry in his suit. He loosens his tie and steps into the room, leaving my now broken door open.

"You need to climb on my face, and you need to wet

those lips, pretty boy, and suck my cock. I have ten minutes until I'm needed back in that meeting."

We both move aside while Enzo strips down naked and climbs onto the bed. Jordyn throws her leg over his head and uses the headboard to hold herself up. "Sit on the bossy asshole's face, Poppet, if he dies, it's one less I have to share you with," Killian says, coming through the doorway.

"I'm about to suck his cock, so if that's not something you're cool with, I suggest you come back for Jordyn in ten minutes."

"Go to town, brother, just keep those lips away from me, and I won't have to kill you."

Killian moves beside the bed and pushes Jordyn's body down onto Enzo's face. "If he can breathe, you're doing it wrong. Grind that pussy right into his face so far he will smell your cunt for the rest of the day."

Dropping down beside them, I angle myself so that I can take his cock in my mouth. I run my tongue over the slit, licking off the small bead of pre-cum, enjoying the way he twists the sheet between his fingers.

Jordyn's mewls of pleasure fill the air, and when they stop, I think she has come again, but as I glance up, I see Kill standing on the end of the bed, his cock in her mouth. Enzo uses both of his hands to keep her moving while I make sure every inch of his cock is looked after.

Never in a million years did I think all three of us would share a woman. Enzo hinted at us sharing a few times, but Kill always turned him down, and I might have thought about it but never acted on it, and I'm glad I didn't until now.

"Oh, shit!" Jordyn screams. Looking up, Kill now has his

cock in his own hand, pumping himself, while Enzo grinds Jordyn's hips into his face. "Don't stop, fuck!!!"

Kill comes at the same time Jordyn does, and then he wipes his hand on his jeans and quickly helps support her body weight. Enzo coughs and splutters, his cock still in my mouth. I cup his balls, and once Jordyn is off his face, he half sits up and watches me. His entire face is fucking wet.

"Did she?"

He nods and has the biggest shit-eating grin on his face. Sucking him in deep and hard, his balls jump and his shaft pulsates in my mouth. Warm liquid squirts down my throat, and I swallow and pull back.

"Now, I have to get back to work," Enzo says, climbing off the bed and picking up his boxer briefs. "If you do that to me again, I will make Kill chain you both up in the basement and edge the fuck out of you until you both can't take it, and then I will do it over and over again."

Jordyn laughs, "That doesn't sound like a punishment."

"I have to agree," I say, flopping down on the bed beside her. Kill stands beside Jordyn and looks down at her like she is his entire reason for living.

"Me either," he says.

"Now, I have to sneak back into my meeting. Sarge, meet me downstairs at six."

I nod. Jordyn looks between us as Enzo leaves the room.

"What's happening at six?" she asks.

I take a deep breath and brace myself for the argument. "We are meeting Lev to negotiate your sister's return."

She narrows her eyes at me. "I'm coming."

I sigh. "Enzo won't let you go. You're pregnant with his

child, and if anyone did anything stupid, we will end up in a bloodbath."

"Poppet, please don't make me go, I hate that bar. If I cause one more fight, I will be banned for life."

She crosses her arms over her belly and pouts. "I'm going, and if you don't take me, I will just find a way to go myself or better yet, I will escape and go to Lev's house myself."

Fuck me, it looks like she is coming, and Enzo can suck it up because he should have kept his mouth shut.

CHAPTER TWELVE

ENZO

Fuck, I hate going to Queen Bee's bar. The establishment is run-down, the floor is always sticky, and the bikers are rowdy and smell like they haven't showered in their lifetime. And, to make matters worse, I have to dress down. There is a literal rule that says no suits allowed.

There is no reason I should be forced into wearing jeans, a T-shirt, and Converse. They're the most uncomfortable shoes known to man and squash my toes. The jeans and shirt belong to Kill, and the shoes are Sarge's. There is no way I would be caught dead in a pair of Kill's combat boots.

One last look in the mirror, and I sigh in annoyance. It will have to do. I head downstairs, where everyone should be waiting in the foyer.

"Wait," Jordyn says. "Who are you, and what did you do with my husband?"

I flip her off and take the last handful of stairs two at a time while Jordyn laughs at my expense.

"Damn, you look hot in a suit, edible in gray sweats, but this? Holy fuck, you look normal."

Sarge snorts from beside her. All four of us are dressed similarly, which agitates the fuck out of me. Kaser and Craig have also dressed down and are coming with us since I knew Jordyn would want to come. They have one job, to make sure she and my son are safe.

"The rules. Don't do anything stupid, don't pick fights, or cause a scene. Bee runs a tight ship, and it's the only place we can meet on neutral ground. Keep close to us, do not wander off, even to go to the bathroom. All the men in that place are loyal to Venom, not us."

"Got it, so I guess I should leave this behind," she says, reaching into her boot and pulling out a knife.

"No, keep it, just in case. None of us have weapons, it's not allowed inside the bar."

She slips it back into her boot.

We all take Sarge's SUV, and Kaser and Craig follow behind us. They will enter the bar first and fit into the crowd, then we will go in after them.

The bar is on the outskirts of town, not far from the Python's compound. Bee inherited the bar from her uncle when he passed away. How someone so cute and peppy ended up with Venom is beyond me.

It takes us just under half an hour to get to the bar; bikes line the curb, and the music is easily heard as we pull up.

Sarge is the first one out. He opens the door for Jordyn and helps her from the SUV. Jordyn walks in step with me toward the bar, and both Kill and Sarge walk in behind us. I head to the bar to let Bee know we are here. She whistles and tells someone to turn the music down.

"Look who the cat dragged in," she drawls.

"It's lovely to see you again, Bee."

Bee laughs. "Enzo, you know you're welcome here anytime, that one, on the other hand," she says, pointing to Kill. He raises his hands.

"I come in peace. I'm just here to make sure nothing happens to Jordyn."

Bee's eyes move to Jordyn, and she smiles. "Yes, I heard you got married. Oh my gosh!"

Bee jumps and launches herself over the bar and places her hands on Jordyn's stomach.

"Never thought I would see the day Enzo settled down and had a family. Did you blackmail him? I figured if blackmail was on the table, it would be that wretched woman. I hate when she comes here and tries to fuck our men."

"No blackmail. Just the flu and I forgot to take my pill."

"That's why I have the bar in my arm. Could you imagine pushing out Venom's babies?"

"Which one is Venom?" Jordyn asks, and Bee points to her man, who sits at the end of the bar. Jordyn's eyes go wide.

"Holy shit, he is like the Hulk, and you're so tiny."

Jordyn blushes, and Bee laughs. "Lev is out the back already; I don't need to tell you to behave."

She looks at another man, one whose name I can't remember. Word on the street is Bee also has a few men on the go. No one really asks questions because Venom would kill them.

"Thanks, Bee, we should just be in and out tonight."

Bee nods, and I lead us to the back of the bar. It used to be a beer garden, and now it's been built in and used for meetings just like this. Bee gets a nice payment for allowing us to use her establishment; I called the meeting, so I have to pay.

When I push through the backdoor that leads to the room, Lev is already seated, and two of his men stand behind him.

Lev's eyes zoom in on Kill. His jaw goes hard, but he doesn't say anything. He knows the drill here.

"You wanted this meet, so what do you want, Enzo? We are busy men."

I shake my head; he really thinks he has the upper hand here. "You know what we want, Lev, the girl."

Lev laughs, "She isn't my prisoner. If you knew what happened to her, maybe you would understand."

"Understand what?" Jordyn snaps. "That a young girl went through something traumatic and has a trauma bond with you? Pfft, you're the adult."

"What the fuck is a trauma bond?" Lev asks.

"It's a response to abuse. Normally, the person who abused them, but you were not innocent in this whole thing. You clearly knew there were kids there, and she is clinging to you because maybe you were the one to show her a tiny slither of niceness."

"Maybe, maybe not."

Doll moves closer and Kill puts his arm out to stop her. "She is a child, not even thirteen. Do you really want to be responsible for her well-being, and what do you plan on doing when she throws herself at you? Are you going to fuck her and tell her everything is okay?"

Lev stands and leans over the table; Sarge and I move closer to Jordyn. "I would never touch a child," he seethes.

"Does she know that? Because I would really hate for

those accusations to be made. It could really ruin a man's reputation," I say. We may be split by families, but there is a bigger divide. Those who fuck with kids and those who don't.

"Please give me my sister back, she is the only person I have ever lived for. Do you know what that's like, or have you been lucky to have a family? Because we don't; we only have each other. Everything I have done since I was nine years old has been for that girl. I just want my family back."

Tears run down her cheeks with every word. Lev doesn't look affected, and I wouldn't expect him to be. This was a long shot.

"And my father's dead, and I guess he is never coming back." Lev doesn't give a fuck that his father is dead. He made that clear already. It's a move to make Jordyn feel bad for something she didn't do.

Kill steps forward, and I brace myself to stop him. "I would say I'm sorry, but I'm not. It's kill or be killed, you know that. Don't take your beef with me out on her. Name a time and place, and I will be there; we can fight to the death."

Lev snorts. "Not even I'm stupid enough to fight you to the death. It does give me an idea, though. The Aces crew runs an underground fight club. Everyone is there, the Irish, the Pythons, it's a free-for-all. If Enzo can fight me and win, the girl is yours."

Of course, he would underestimate me. Kill is bat shit crazy, and Sarge was my bodyguard, but what he fails to realize is that I taught Sarge everything he knows. I grew up in the same life he did, we learned to fight as soon as we could walk.

"Why me?" I ask curiously.

"Just because I would get satisfaction from hitting your pretty boy face and the money, of course."

"Fine, get us on the sheet for Saturday night. When I win, the girl comes home with me."

"And if you lose, what do I get?"

"Me," Killian says, taking a step forward.

Lev smirks. "You have yourself a deal."

We don't bother with pleasantries; we leave the same way we came. It's not until we are back at the car that Sarge punches Kill in the face.

"What the fuck is your problem?" Kill snaps, rubbing his jaw.

"You. Why would you fucking risk working for them? You know there is a good chance Lev could take Enzo. I have seen him fight, and he is as good."

Kill shakes his head. "Because he won't keep me around, he is scared of me. I will be used as a trade, and you know who wants me. Ronan O'Brien."

"Why the fuck would he want you?" I ask. He looks down. "Kill, fucking answer me."

"He is my cousin. My mother was his father's sister. She was a disgrace to the family for having me with a man from a rival family. When my parents died, and I was sent away, no one came for me, but Ronan must have found out somehow that we are related, and he wants me to come and work for him, but I have other plans. I want them to suffer, just like I had to."

They all get into the SUV, but I need a few moments to compose myself. How the fuck did I not know this? I make sure I know everything about everyone I surround myself with. The only way this could have gotten past me is the Feds. Everything inside me says Killian wouldn't be working with them, but I never imagined Leo was either.

It makes me wonder if I should throw the fight. There are other ways to get the kid back. Lev will get bored with her soon enough and send her back.

CHAPTER THIRTEEN

JORDYN

Enzo and Sarge have been in the gym a lot more than usual this week. I don't know if I should be pissed at Killian or thankful that he is risking himself for my sister. I have no doubt that whatever twisted bullshit plan Killian has will lead him right back here, and it's a big if. Enzo has to lose first.

After I finish peeing for what feels like the hundredth time today, I wash my hands and squeal when I see a shadow out of the corner of my eye.

"For fuck's sake, Killian, stop sneaking up on me. My bladder isn't what it used to be, and I don't enjoy wetting myself."

"Have you been avoiding me?" he asks as I step out of the ensuite in Enzo's room. I have been sleeping in here because Milo has taken up residence in my bedroom.

"Yes," I answer honestly. He looks at me like he wasn't expecting me to say yes. "I don't know if I should be mad at you or thankful. I miss Pixie so damn much, but I also don't know how I would feel about you not being here."

"Poppet, trust me. I need to do this. Enzo will not win that fight against Lev, and I need an in with the Irish without willingly going in. Please trust that I know what I'm doing. Pixie will be returned to you by the morning."

"Why won't Enzo win the fight, he isn't going to throw it, is he?"

Killian sits on the bed and pats the spot beside him. "I have known Enzo for a long time, and he will be in a war with himself. He wants to get Pixie back for you because even if he won't admit it, he is crazy about you. He will also be questioning everything I have ever told him; my background check has no information on me being related to them. My parents were in witness protection, and when they died, someone ordered for me to be sent to that place, and I need to know who so I can finish my list.

"There is a lot that I haven't told anyone about my past, including Enzo. Ronan wants me to do a job for him, one I'm not willing to do unless forced. I need some intel to find out who killed my mother. Once the job is done, he won't need me anymore, and I will be back. You won't even notice that I'm gone."

Leaning in, I wrap my arms around him. He goes stiff in my hold, but I don't care, I just squeeze him tighter until his arms wrap around me. "Please be safe."

"Trust me, I will be, because I plan to come back. I feel things right now that I can't act on because of the baby. Once he is out of you, all bets are off."

Pulling back, a tear rolls down my face. Killian uses his thumb to wipe it, and he licks the wetness from his finger. "I just don't understand why he will throw the fight. If he wins, we can all be happy."

"It's to test my loyalty. If I come back, he can trust me, and we both know he is bull-headed. Just know Pixie is coming home, and I will be back as soon as I can."

Someone knocks on the door, interrupting the moment. Sarge pops his head in. "We need to leave, soo... What's wrong?"

He steps into the room and squats down in front of me, using a finger under my chin to make me look at him. "Killian told me Enzo is going to throw the fight."

Sarge cuts a glare to Killian. "You don't know that. Why make her upset?"

"I do know it. This is Enzo we are talking about. He has to do what is right for the family, even if he doesn't want to, and after everything with his parents and Leo, he should have killed me on the spot for not telling him."

"He might surprise you, let's have a little faith and support him either way."

I reluctantly let Sarge pull me to my feet. "Let's go and get this over with."

My stomach is massive. I feel like a beached whale all the time, nothing fits right, and I'm uncomfortable. I stick to my original statement and still don't understand why people do this to themselves more than once.

When we exit Enzo's room and pass my old room, Milo wheels himself out. "Let's go," he says, and Killian holds his arm out.

"Where the fuck do you think you're going? You need to heal because when I get back, I'm going to have fun torturing your ass."

Milo pouts. "Are you going on vacation?"

"Something like that," Kill mutters.

"Can I still come?"

"No," both Sarge and Killian say at the same time. Milo snaps at them but wheels himself back into his room.

When we get downstairs, Enzo is waiting, dressed in his suit, holding a small sports bag in his hand. "When we get there, you stay beside Kaser all night, no matter what happens. You risk my son's life, and I will kill you myself."

"Calm down, he is my son as well, and I would never do anything to risk his life. I want my sister back, and if she is there, then so am I."

"I'm sorry. I'm on edge because this is a place where families go to fight their enemies. Fights can break out at any time. It's heavily guarded, but I don't want anything happening to you."

The front door opens, and Angelo steps inside, wearing a suit, and it's a stark difference from every other time I have seen him. "How do I look, do I fit the underboss role? I mean, if you die tonight, I will take your place, right?"

"Fuck you," Enzo snaps, and Angelo laughs.

"I'm kidding, bro, but we need to start showing a united front, and I want to try. This is as much my birthright as yours. Papa says to not be an idiot. He and our uncles are currently drinking themselves into a coma, talking about the good old days."

Mario decided a few days ago to stay with Angelo, claiming Enzo is starting a family and doesn't need his father hanging around all the time.

Enzo, Sarge, Killian, and I go to the garage, and all get into Sarge's SUV. Kaser and his men are already at the warehouse where the fights are held. Enzo wanted them to be familiar with the place by the time that we got there. Angelo takes his own car, mainly because Enzo doesn't really trust his motives yet.

The ride to the place is intense. Enzo is quiet in the front seat, and Killian sits quietly with his hand on my leg while Sarge keeps looking at me from the rear-view mirror.

As we pull into a parking lot, my mouth falls open. I don't know what I was expecting but motorbikes line the entrance, a fleet of black Jeeps are parked on one side of the lot, flashy sports cars in another, and there are SUVs with blacked-out windows.

In my head, this place would be run and filled with low-level gang bangers, but this place is filled with criminals, just not of the variety I grew up with. These men have money and lots of it, so it makes me wonder why they even bother with this place, especially if everyone is enemies.

Killian must see me gawking out the window. "The Jeeps are the Irish. Fuckers all think they are cool and untouchable, and the sports cars will be the Margaux family."

"Who?" I ask. That isn't a name that I'm familiar with.

"They own the racetrack and run the gambling for this area."

I nod. "And the bikes? I can tell some would be the Pythons."

"That would be the Aces crew, they run this place."

Jesus, there is so much more to this world than I expected. I was so naïve on my side of town that I just thought the worst there was were junkies and drug dealers. Boy, was I wrong about that. Trafficking, gambling rings, fancy clubs, money. Thinking of it all at once overwhelms me.

Sarge parks and gets out of the car, coming around to open my door. I take his hand, and as I slip out, I see Kaser and a team of men, along with Angelo, two men that are Enzo's second cousins, and Charlotte walking towards us.

"What is she doing here?" Enzo snaps, and Angelo smirks at him and shrugs.

"Excuse me! I'm grown, and you can't tell me what to do. I came because I want Pix back as much as Jordyn does. If you don't win this fight, I will tell all the aunts, and they will rain down hell on you. Head of the family or not."

Enzo takes a step toward Charlotte and scowls down at her, but she doesn't flinch. "I will do what the fuck I want, and you will do as you're told. That's how this works. Stay with Angelo, or I will have your ass thrown out. Do you understand me?"

She rolls her eyes. "Yes, Dad."

We walk in a group to the door, and security waves us in. Enzo leads us up a set of stairs to a mezzanine, and it looks like each family has their own. Punters downstairs are placing bets while topless women serve drinks. I expected the inside to look run-down, but this place is far from that.

Old-school rap music fills the air, along with a haze of smoke that smells like weed.

Once we are at the top, I take a seat, and Sarge sits to my left. We have a perfect view of the fight going on downstairs. Two men in boots, jeans, and no shirts throw punches. One lands a solid fist to his jaw, and blood fills his mouth, his grin now red.

Sarge leans in close. "The guy with his hair tied back is

Darragh, and the other is Cian, been best friends for as long as I have been here."

Turning away from the men beating the shit out of each other, I look at Sarge. "Why are they fighting each other?"

Sarge shrugs as Killian takes a seat on my right. "They are crazy fucks, always beating the crap out of each other for one reason or another. Ronan only allows it here; he can't have a rift between any of his men. The Irish fucks only ever fight each other, which is smart. There is no bad blood with other families. They might spout the bullshit that what happens here stays here, but it doesn't. It spills out, and grudges are held. It's why Enzo rarely lets anyone fight here. He believes it's beneath the family name to be involved."

"Because it is," Enzo says from behind me. "Fighting like this is barbaric and unnecessary. Airing your grievances in public."

"So why fight Lev?"

Enzo places his hands on my shoulders and gives a light squeeze. "You're the mother of my child, and getting your sister back is important to you, so it's important to me."

"More important than proving Killian's loyalty?" I ask with my head tilted back and a brow raised.

"Yes," he says through gritted teeth.

Killian stands. "If it eases your worries, I'm going with Ronan either way. He is out for blood, and we all know that blood attracts predators, not prey, Enzo. I have unresolved shit with my family. My loyalty is always with you, but this needs to be done. When I get back, you can hand out whatever punishment you see fit, but I will not bring a war to our doorstep, not when we have more to lose now. Jordyn, Pixie, and Mars are my priority. I need you to have faith, just like I did almost six years ago when you asked me to work for you."

Enzo's eyes soften, and he nods. He won't stop Killian; he knows he can't, but Killian has a lot to answer for when he gets back, and I hope he is willing to answer Enzo's questions. This will feel like a betrayal and won't be an easy wound to heal.

The MC announces Cian as the winner. He picks up Darragh and throws him over his shoulder, slapping his best mate's ass as the crowd parts for them. I gasp.

"Is that?"

All of my men look down and see what I do. Harper is in a very tight and very short dress, standing beside Ronan and another man, with a smile on her face as she looks up at him. He says something, and she laughs. Cian stops beside her, grabs her face with his bloody hand, and kisses her.

Oh no, this isn't good. She has caught feelings for these men, and it could mean the end of our friendship. Unless she is a way better actress than I give her credit for.

"Fuck, is that your friend?" Charlotte asks. "Does she know who they are?"

Angelo scoffs from beside her. "She is a whore, she doesn't care who they are as long as they pay."

Charlotte slaps Angelo. "She is a mattress actress actually, have some respect for a woman who does what she has to. Where would you be without your daddy's money or your brother's protection?"

"Harper is a big girl, and the same could have been said about me. It's not like your family is the epitome of innocence, either."

Enzo moves his hand around my throat and leans down,

his mouth resting below my ear. "But you love my cock, don't you, Doll? It makes you forget all about how bad of a man I really am."

I try to act like his words don't affect me, but wetness pools between my legs.

"D'Arco!" someone yells, and Enzo slowly turns. "You're up after this fight, you need to get ready."

Sarge stands and places a kiss on top of my head. "I'm going down with Enzo, stay up here with Kill."

Both Enzo and Sarge head downstairs to get ready. "Once his fight starts, Poppet, I have to leave, so please stay up here with Kaser and Angelo. I know you hate him, but you are his brother's wife, and he will protect you with his life."

"Do you really have to go?" I pout.

He nods his head yes. "I need to know what he wants with me. At least, this way, I could get some answers about my parents, and if I need to kill them all, I will, but I won't be back until it's safe."

"Just make sure Harper doesn't get hurt in your plan, she is like a sister to me."

Killian nods. We sit in silence through the next fight between a guy from the Pythons MC and a massive Russian.

My heart hurts, knowing damn well there is a slight chance that he is never coming back. His need to get vengeance against everyone who hurt him gives him tunnel vision.

CHAPTER FOURTEEN

KILLIAN

As soon as Enzo steps into the ring, I make my exit. I don't need him to make it any harder for me to leave. He only has a small idea about what I went through as a child. They tortured us when we were naughty or didn't follow exact directions, and as I grew, I pushed back hard, and my punishments were harsher than the kids around me.

After a while, I started to see some of the other kids were smiling. With the attention on me, they had a chance to have a small slither of happiness. I became numb to the pain inflicted on me after some time, and they had to start getting inventive. It wasn't enough that they took in children and trained us to become killers. They dumped us in the wilderness and played a game very similar to the Hunger Games. The similarity is the winner was the last one standing.

We were fucking tagged like animals and tracked. Once we were deemed worthy enough, they started taking us on field trips, where we were given a photo and knew what had to be done. The kicker was when they gave us a time limit and strapped a vest of explosives on us. If we didn't hit our mark and get back to the van, it was kaboom. Some days I walked back to the van, wondering how nice it would be to no longer have to survive. But Cal made me make a pact that we would get stronger and kill them all. We did. Every last one of them and anyone who dared to fight for them. The rest possibly ran; I don't know exactly what happened to them. I didn't really care, no one was allowed to make friends in there. Even Cal and I had to pretend for years, or they would have pitted us against each other.

Ronan and his entourage leave through the back entrance, Harper by his side. I keep to the shadows and make my way around the back of all the Jeeps. Fucking a waste of money if you ask me.

Slipping between two cars, Ronan steps out, and I smirk. I wondered how long it would take him to notice I was following.

"I can see you have come to your senses," he smirks.

"Some could argue I was never in my right mind."

Ronan bellows out a laugh. "Must run in the family."

I force out a laugh, this man is no family to me, I will let him believe what he wants. Cian comes around with Harper thrown over his shoulder, her ass out for everyone to see, and she giggles. Cian sets her down on her feet, and her mouth forms an O when she realizes it's me standing here. Cian tries to step in front of her in a protective move, but she swats him away.

"Stop it, I know him. Is everything okay with Dolly?" she asks. I realize now her smart move, using her nickname for Jordyn.

"Who is Dolly?" Ronan asks.

"A girl I work with at The Range. Kill is a regular between her legs. Isn't that right?"

I nod. "Is everything good here?" Cian asks Ronan.

"It is, take the girl home. I have some business to take care of, and I will join you later."

The Jeeps start leaving one by one, and Ronan presses a fob, and his lights flash. "You going to kill me on the drive over?"

I shrug. "I thought about it, but I decided to hear you out like you asked. If I don't like what you have to say, I make no promises."

Ronan laughs. "When I tell you what I know, I won't be the only one you want to kill."

I nod. If he just had information, I don't understand why he would want to bring me back into the family. Something more is going on, and I plan to find out what.

He pulls into a gated community; security opens the gates for him, and he drives until there is no road left and pulls into the driveway of a modern mansion. This estate was newly built in the last few years.

More security greets us when we exit the car. "Sorry, we need to pat you down."

I sigh. "Just know whoever pats me down will die. It might not be today, but once you're on my list, your fate is sealed."

The men hesitate, and Ronan pushes them out of the way and uses his boot to kick my legs open. "You're already threatening death, and you haven't even been inside the house yet."

He pats me down, and when he takes my blade from my

boot, I growl, "Put it in the car, I want that back. It's my favorite killin' knife."

"You will get it back, calm down. The next part you won't like all that much, so let's get it over with."

I follow Ronan and his men up the front stairs and into the house, and down into their basement. It's a lot more modern and less ready for killing to happen, so that is a relief. I guess the Irish don't do their work at home.

"So, I guess you don't kill your enemies down here."

Ronan shakes his head. "I personally don't like to get my hands dirty. I'm squeamish, and blood, on occasion, makes me faint. Just like your boss, I have someone who does the dirty work for me."

He motions for me to sit. "I take it I'm not here to kill anyone for you, then. Are we going to get to the point, or do you want to reminisce about the life you got and the shit hand it dealt me?"

Ronan pours two glasses of whiskey and hands me one before he sits opposite me. "I wouldn't exactly say you have the crappy hand, you're free of this family. But we do need your help with something."

I take a small sip of the whiskey and wait; Ronan has a reputation, and he is very quick to anger. I would like to keep this interaction between us as short as possible.

"Give me the name of who you need me to kill or find, and I will be on my way."

Ronan rolls up the sleeves of his long-sleeve button-up shirt, his style reminding me a lot of Enzo.

"It's not that simple. I need you to hear me out before you do anything stupid. I wouldn't have contacted you if it wasn't important."

Leaning back in the armchair, I cross my legs at the ankles. I may as well hear him out.

"I need you to find Mary Katherine."

Looking up at him, I laugh. Is he fucking with me right now? "I killed that bitch a long time ago."

"Are we really sure of that?" a female voice purrs, and the hairs on the back of my neck stand on end. That is a voice I haven't heard in almost two decades. I stand from my chair, turn, and throw the glass in my hand toward her. She sidesteps and cackles at me.

"That is no way to greet your sister."

I snarl at her like a wild animal. No one in this world, besides Cal and the Irish, knows I have siblings. They're dead to me, but here this traitorous bitch stands. I knew there was a slight possibility she could be here, but I figured they would have killed her, but no such luck. I spared her life once because she was always my weakness, but not anymore. It won't happen again.

Men start to fill the room, their weapons pointed at me. "Why the fuck are you ambushing me like this? Do you remember what I told you the last time I saw you?"

She rolls her eyes at me. It used to be cute when she was a teenager, but now, she is a grown-ass woman and an insult to me—the person who spared her life after what she did to me.

"I need your help, and I knew you wouldn't do it for me."

The doors bang open, and two freckled-faced girls run into the room. "Mommy, save us; there are monsters under the beds here."

The girls stand beside my sister, and one of the girls

looks at me and screams. "Sadie," she whispers. "I think the monster is in here."

Her twin looks up at me, and her eyes go wide. "Boo," I say, making both girls scream. A younger man runs into the room.

"I'm so sorry, they are so fast. I couldn't find them."

The man takes the girls from the room, and my sister locks the door behind them. "Was that really necessary, scaring them like that?"

I shrug. "Seemed fitting. It's not like she was wrong, I am a monster, and you should be afraid."

Ronan clears his throat. "Look, I know my father was an asshole, but he had good reason to go after your father. He took your mother from her family. He couldn't find any of you kids after you were taken into protection."

"Bullshit," I snap. "If they managed to kill my parents, then why the fuck were we sent away? And you really think I'm going to help you after you were part of the reason this fucking happened to me?" I motion to my face. "Yes, my dear sister told Mary Katherine of my plans. My punishment was acid eating away at my skin. I'm lucky that I'm even alive."

"I'm sorry," she sobs.

"Cut the fucking act, Fiona." I snap, her crocodile tears do nothing for me.

Her face morphs, and the real her comes back. "You're right, I'm not sorry for what I did. They promised me freedom, and it was every person for themselves. I was raped day in and day out."

"I know!" I yell. "So the fuck was I, but I never threw you under the bus. I had a plan, one I executed perfectly, might I add. All you had to do was wait a few more weeks;

instead, we were there an extra two years. I didn't see sunlight for over twelve months. Do you know what that does to a person?"

"Look, we understand you don't want to help your sister, but what about her?" Ronan asks, sliding a folder across the coffee table in front of him.

I pick up the folder; there are pictures of my sister's children and Milo, and the very last pictures are Pixie and Jordyn's stomach.

"Who did you leave alive?" Ronan asks.

"Besides us, Cal, Pike..."

"Are you fucking kidding me?! You didn't kill Pike?" Fiona shouts as she paces the room. "You always had a weakness."

"I don't. I killed every fucker I had to so I could escape, but Pike was our brother."

Fiona scoffs. "Our half-brother, who hated our guts our entire lives, Killian. He was their soldier and would have done anything that bitch asked him to. She promised him her daughter."

"Sucks to be him, I slit her throat right in front of him. It's how I knew I wanted to be the 'Cutthroat Killer' as people call me."

"Please help me fix this; I can't have my children in danger. I need your help."

Turning to face the woman who used to be my sister, I shrug. "To be honest, I don't give a shit about your children. Why are you the only one who received the pictures?"

It seems weird to me she would be the only one to get them. If someone is coming after us, it would make more sense if we all received them.

"Because I added the photos of the others. I thought you might help if children you were close with were in danger."

"Fuck you, I'm not helping."

Turning to leave, I come face to face with a gun. I cackle. A bullet hole can't make it worse.

"Please, Killian," she whispers. "Don't let my sins be the reason those girls die." Turning back around to face her, I give her a flat stare. "I was just a kid trying to survive."

She nods at Ronan, who slides another folder across the table. I walk back over and reluctantly sit down. Opening it, I flick through the images, some of Fiona when she was younger in compromising positions, sinner in red across them, pictures of her girls at the park, and a note.

> You're living on borrowed time. You're the weakest link. Your family took something from me, and now, you will pay the ultimate price. An eye for an eye.
> Tik tock, princess, you have until the moon is full.

She then hands me another photo, one with her face scratched out. It was a picture taken not even a week before I killed every adult and child follower. The only people to walk out alive were my siblings, Cal, myself, and some younger children who hadn't been brainwashed yet.

"Why would it be Pike? He is part of our 'family,' and why now, it makes no sense. He seems to live a normal life now with a wife and two children. Have you told anyone about where we grew up?"

"Besides Ronan, no. Who have you told?"

"Enzo knows some details, as does Sarge, but they don't know specifics."

"So, you'll help me?"

"Fuck no. I will pay Pike a visit, but make no mistake, I couldn't care less if your light is snuffed out. Jordyn is my priority, and I won't let my past reach her. So, it looks like you got lucky."

Tears stream down her face. Once upon a time, we were inseparable; we shared a womb, but now she is nothing more than a stranger. Her face saved her from death only because she looked exactly like our mother. I couldn't kill her; I did leave her for dead, but somehow, she ended up here.

"Do you Irish pricks have safe houses?"

Ronan nods. "Get her to one, along with the children. Don't take her in one of your usual vehicles. If you have a delivery that comes in, hide them in that truck or van, then switch them into another car and take them. I will need some time to gather information. Give her a burner phone that only you will know the number to. I will call you to get it... And sister, if I ever see your face again, it will be me you need to be afraid of."

The men lower their weapons, and someone steps forward and unlocks the door. A small human sits at the door. "Are you really a monster?" the child whispers and I squat down in front of her.

"Yes, but not one you need to be afraid of. What's your name?"

"Eloise, my mom says monsters are not real."

I smile at her. "Your mom should stop lying to you."

"Killian," Fiona barks. "She is a child."

Eloise rolls her eyes, the exact same way Fiona does. "I'm almost seven, and she thinks I'm a baby."

"I think seven is very grown up."

Eloise giggles and whispers, "Who did that to your face?"

"That is a story for another time."

She nods, and I push to my feet, turning back to Ronan. "I need a car, something that won't stick out like a sore thumb."

"Kayne, give him the keys to your car. I will buy you a brand new one."

"Yes, boss."

Kayne, one of Ronan's security, hands me the keys to his car. Ronan comes up beside me and walks me out. I don't bother saying goodbye to Fiona, our familial ties died the day my fucking face melted. Ronan takes me to his car, gives me back my knife, and shows me where his staff park their cars. Kayne's car is just a beat-up shit box, and it's perfect for what I need it to do. When I'm pulling out of the estate, I dial Cal.

"You ringing so I can yell at you some more?" he says instead of hello.

"You wish, are you alone?"

I hear him shuffle around. "I am now, I have a lady friend."

I don't know why he feels the need to tell me. "I just saw Fiona."

Cal coughs down the phone. "What the fuck did she want? I hope you killed the bitch this time."

"Not exactly, turns out someone is threatening to kill her."

Cal sighs. "So what? Let them do what you should have all those years ago."

"It's not that simple. They sent photos and a note, but one photo was of all of us: you, me, her, and Pike. One of us could be next. I can't risk Jordyn."

"Fuck, what do you need me to do?"

I take an exit that leads out of town. "Nothing yet, I'm going to pay Pike a visit, they think it might be him."

"Well, you killed his woman in front of him. I wouldn't let your friends find out that information."

"I have no intention of telling them. I will send a message to Sarge to double security, and Milo is safe."

Cal scoffs. "It's not like he can go anywhere after you broke his fucking legs."

"He knew the risks, and he still kept coming back. I swear I wasn't going to hurt him that much, but he pissed my woman off, and she got him good. I can assure you his legs are only slightly fractured. Anyway, you didn't tell anyone about our time..."

"Of course, I didn't. Milo knows small snippets, but I don't make a habit of telling people my life story. It's not something I like to relive."

"I had to ask, you know...to eliminate suspects. Something is going on, and I plan to find out."

"Keep me updated."

He ends the call, and I do the same. Pike lives a few hours away. I really have no desire to see the prick, but I think a nice family reunion is in order.

CHAPTER FIFTEEN

SARGE

Killian called me three days ago and told me to tighten security around Jordyn and Milo. He wouldn't say why except to trust him. Pixie was returned the night of the fight, and she and Jordyn had a massive fight.

Apparently, she loves Lev, and because she interfered, he won't ever love her back. Of course, Jordyn tried explaining that it's not right for someone his age to like a child, which sparked a screaming match about her not being a child. Then she met Milo, and she has been annoying him, which works out well for us.

My phone vibrates from beside me; I hate that my bed is empty and can't wait for the new wing to be ready. At least then, with what Enzo has in store, we can all be close. I know they would let me sleep with them, but I feel like I'm intruding on their time.

"Hello," I say, answering the call from a private number.

"Help me! Please."

"Missy?"

It can't be, I must be having a nightmare. The call ends. I'm slightly shaken and get out of bed. It's not like I could sleep anyway; I never do when Jordyn isn't beside me.

Throwing on a pair of sweats, I head down to the kitchen for breakfast. Normally, I would have been up and in the gym, but I felt so damn fatigued I thought I would skip the morning workout and go for a run in the afternoon.

The smell of coffee wafts through the house, which means Jordyn has snuck out of bed and is sneaking a cup before Enzo tips it all down the sink. He has tried tricking her into drinking decaf, and it isn't working out well for him.

She has her back to me, and I perv on her ass for a few minutes as she shakes it to a Lizzo song. Sneaking in behind her, I wrap my arms around her stomach, and she squeals, whacking me in the arm.

"Sarge, you scared the shit out of me."

Having her in my arms grounds me. The call was weird, but I don't want to worry her about it. I don't know who would play such a shitty joke, but I plan to ask a buddy to see if they can pinpoint where the call came from.

"You know Enzo has the nose of a bloodhound and will be down here any second now."

"He won't, I bought a coffee-scented candle and put it in our room a few days ago, so now he just thinks it's that, and I get one cup in before I shower, then I blow him, and he asks no questions."

"Speaking of blowing," I joke, and she turns in my arms and kisses my chest.

"Are." kiss. "You." kiss. "Jealous?"

Her hand slides down the front of my sweats, and she wraps her hand around my cock.

"Why don't you come upstairs and shower with us?"

"Oh God," I say as her hand strokes me. "As much as I want to, I can't. I have to go out."

"Well then, you better be on the lookout."

Jordyn falls to her knees, using me to get her down without falling over, and she shimmies my sweats down my legs. Wasting no time, she wraps her lips around me. I use my hand to brace myself against the kitchen counter. She takes me deep into the back of her throat, and my eyes close.

"As much as I normally would just stand and watch, there is a pint-sized princess on her way down here, and I need you to hide me."

Opening my eyes, Jordyn pops off my cock, and I grumble about it not being fair. Jordyn giggles and pulls my sweats back up, and when she holds out her hand to me, I help pull her to her feet.

"Milo!" Pixie yells. His eyes go wide, and he takes off on his crutches. When Pixie comes into the kitchen, she runs her eyes over us.

"Have you seen Milo?" I shake my head no.

She sighs and starts to leave before she stops. "Oh, Catalina is here. She went upstairs."

"Go," I say. Jordyn's face is red, and she is mad. Cat has no idea what she is about to do by going upstairs. I wouldn't be surprised if Enzo throws the bitch down a flight of stairs.

Jordyn mumbles insults under her breath as I follow behind her, but I stop off quickly at my room. Enzo won't let anything happen to her while I throw on a shirt and a pair of sneakers.

Once I leave my room, a scream from Enzo's room

catches my attention, and I rush up to his room and push the door open. Jordyn is sitting on Catalina's back.

Enzo watches on with a smirk on his face. "She took her down," is all he says.

"Pass me your gun!" she shouts. "If this bitch has no clothes on under her coat, she is dead."

"Enzo, get your wife's fat ass off me."

Grinding my teeth together, I take a step toward the women until I'm pulling Jordyn off of Cat.

"I'm going to kill her," Jordyn seethes, and I chuckle in her ear. That is something I would pay to watch.

Enzo leans down, grabs Cat by her silky blonde hair, and drags her to her feet. She is facing us with Enzo at her back. He pulls her to his chest.

"Open the coat, Cat, and show my wife what is underneath."

The crocodile tears start. "No, I won't."

Enzo leans in closer to her ear, and just above a whisper, he says, "If you don't, I will let Kill take you downstairs and not even give your family a chance to say goodbye. We are no longer friends, you're no longer welcome in mine and my wife's home. Events, galas, family gatherings, if I see you, I will put a bullet in your head."

Enzo reaches around her body and starts unbuttoning her coat. When he is done, he slides the material off her shoulders and lets it fall to the floor, and she has nothing on underneath. Jordyn tries to free herself from my hold. The vile words that spew from her mouth make my cock hard, and I immediately know it's a big mistake. She turns slightly, and I let her turn to face me. She pushes at my chest.

"If seeing her naked makes your cock hard, you can fucking leave with her."

Smiling at her is also a terrible mistake when her hand connects with my face. Her mouth forms an O when she realizes she has hit me. She crumbles in my arms, and I slowly help her to the ground, keeping her wrapped in my arms.

"MILO!" Enzo shouts. When he walks through the door, his eyes go wide as saucers when he takes in a naked woman in the room.

"When I joked about poly life, I didn't mean with you. No offense, but you're all old."

Jordyn laughs hysterically. "I don't want to fuck you, kid. I need you to escort Cat from the house and make sure she gets in her car and leaves."

Milo nods. "That I can do. I thought you wanted me to bang her, and she is way too skinny and plastic for my taste. Let's go, Barbie, I have a teenage girl to hide from."

Enzo releases Cat and shoves her toward Milo. He is walking better now, which is good, all things considered. I'm sure he should have casts on still, but he refused them.

"Take this," Enzo says, handing Milo a Glock. "That is now yours, lose it and find out what happens. Kill someone with it, you bring it to me or Sarge."

Milo nods. "And is she leaving naked?" Enzo nods. "Okay, Blondie, let's get going."

"You're going to regret this," Cat seethes. "I came to give you one last chance to come to your senses."

Enzo shakes his head; Cat leaves the room with her head held high. If only she realized she has nothing on Jordyn. The size of your body isn't what makes you beautiful. Yes,

Cat has a killer body, but Jordyn's curves are fucking spectacular, and she has thighs I want to be trapped between every day.

"Doll, are you okay?" Enzo asks. She buries her head further into me.

"I can't do this anymore. I'm not that person who attacks other women over a man. Even though you sent her away, if she ever comes back, I'm done."

"Look at me," Enzo demands, and Jordyn looks up at him, blinking through her tears. He cups her face and uses his thumbs to wipe them away. "No other woman will ever compare to you. Yes, our situation is unconventional, and things have been rocky since you came back, but I'm sick of fighting it. You're it for me, and so are you," he says, looking at me. "Neither of you will have to share me with anyone else except yourselves. I'm crazy about the both of you. You're all I think about, and it drives me insane. If I'm being honest, I'm jealous of the bond you and Kill have, and the bond you both have. I know I'm a little bit of a pain."

Jordyn snorts. "A little, you think?" Enzo smiles. "I'm sorry about your mom. I know the things she did were inexcusable, but she was still your mother, and I honestly didn't mean to hurt her. After being interrogated, sent home by myself, and she... I swear she had a gun, or at least made me believe that she did. I would never have..."

"Shh, I know. I needed someone to blame, and it was a relief once I found out what she was doing. Let's all move on, my father is back, Pixie is home..."

"Kill will be back," I add, and Enzo looks at me, and I can see the uncertainty in his eyes. He isn't sure, but I know him, and I know he loves Jordyn. There is no way that he isn't coming back. Enzo helps Jordyn up and asks her if she would like a bath. When my phone buzzes in my pocket, I leave them to bond a little and step out of the room, answering the call from an unknown number.

"I love you, Sergeant, to the moon and stars."

The phone slips from my fingers. Hearing her voice sends me back to the day she died.

"I love you, Missy!" I scream as tears roll down my face. Two men hold me back, but I keep my eyes on hers, and tears roll down her face as the man thrusts inside her.

"I love you, Sergeant, to the moon and the stars."

Bile sits in my throat as he moves out of her and stands, walking around her body. He kneels and grips his cock, stroking it until he comes on her lips. He reaches for his knife, and my vision blurs.

"Missy!"

Everything goes black when the blade moves across her throat.

CHAPTER SIXTEEN

JORDYN

It's been over two weeks since Killian left. Sarge and Enzo have no idea where he is, and he hasn't tried to contact me. Everything here has been quiet...way too quiet if you ask me. Sarge has been a little distant, and I can't pinpoint what's wrong. Mario is in and out with his two brothers, and they are hell-bent on finding Aldo.

Pixie is slowly coming around, even if she has her sights set on Milo, who is still too old for her. I don't know why she feels the need to want a boy in her life right now. She refuses to talk to me about what happened to her.

The upside to today is that the nursery furniture has arrived, and Enzo has security unloading it into the house while I sit at the bottom of the stairs with all three dogs by my side. Mutley half sits on my lap and the stairs, while Balthazar and Ansel sit on either side of me. I run my fingers over Mutley's coarse fur. When one of the young security guards comes in with a box and approaches, Ansel stands and growls, and Balthazar moves closer to me.

"This box came for you in the mail."

It's only a small box, nothing larger than what you'd get in the standard mail. Sarge whistles, and both Ansel and Balthazar stand down. I move Mutley from my lap and push to my feet, meeting the poor man where he stands so the dogs don't rip him apart.

Sarge calls the dogs, and all three start to follow him, which is smart. It's probably safer if he puts them in their room.

"Thank you," I say to the young man whose name I think is Cam, but there are so many of them, I can never remember who is who. I take the package, rip off the tape, and open the lid. The box is filled with pictures of Harper, covered in blood. I drop the box, and Kaser comes running toward me.

"Someone call Harper. NOW!!!"

Milo is next to race down the stairs; he must not know what's happening. "Jordyn, you need to come and see Pixie, now."

I nod. "Kaser, find Harper, please. I need to know that she is okay."

"On it, go and check on your sister."

Milo rips his shirt off and hands it to me. "To wipe your hands."

Taking the shirt, I wipe the sticky red from my hands, and I notice it's not thick enough to be actual blood. I follow him up to Pixie's room, where she sits on her bed and holds out her phone.

"You lied to me," she says. "You told me Mom was missing, but she looks alive to me."

Moving closer, I take the phone from her hands and

scroll through the pictures of our mother. She looks healthy. A drastic change from the last I saw of her.

"I said she was missing, not dead, Pix. I seriously had no idea where she was."

The better question is, who the hell is sending her pictures of our mother? This makes no sense.

Enzo and Sarge come storming into the room. Enzo takes the phone from my hand.

"You might need to talk to Kill about that...she was brought in with Alek. Kaser has gone to Harper's apartment because she isn't answering her phone."

"We need to talk," Sarge says. "In private."

"I will stay with Pixie," Milo says, and I nod. Right now, I don't have any answers for her. Enzo takes us down to his office, and when he opens the door, Killian sits in his office chair with his boots up on his desk. He kicks his legs off and stands. My body connects hard with his, and he stumbles back a little.

"Miss me, Poppet?"

Pulling back, I look at his face and then pull him back in again. He just stands there and takes my affection; I know he will hate it, and that's fine.

"Where have you been?"

"I can fill you in later. Sarge sent me an SOS message last week, and I had a few loose ends I needed to tie up. I can't..."

"If you tell me you're not staying, I'm going to murder you myself." He laughs at me. "And why did you send an SOS?"

We all sit. "I needed Kill back because I needed everyone here for what I had to say, but firstly. How did you conveniently know to be here right now? You have been in the basement, haven't you?"

Killian shrugs. "Guilty, I needed the use of the back rooms, and I didn't want to be disturbed."

"Can we focus?" Enzo snaps. "One thing at a damn time. Sarge, you go first."

Sarge nods and takes a deep breath. "I have been getting phone calls from Missy."

We all freeze. Enzo opens his mouth and closes it again. "I know it's not possible. I buried her myself, but it's her voice. But a week ago, I was sent some photos of her, ones from the crime scene."

"Okay, we will get your phone to Cassidy, the head of our IT department, and have him send someone to look into where the calls are coming from. Now, Kill, where the fuck have you been, and can I trust you?"

"If you have to ask me that, then maybe I shouldn't be here."

"Just answer his question," I say, and Kill nods at me.

"I'm only telling this story once. I have a twin sister and an older half-brother. We were all sent away together after our parents died. Pike hated us our entire lives, and we were never close, but Fiona was my other half until she betrayed me to save herself. I lost half my face because of her. Ronan wanted to talk to me because Fiona was sent some photos, and well, I have some old family shit to deal with. When I went to find Pike, I found his wife and children dead, and he was nowhere to be found. Now, he is in the basement."

"Okay, Jordyn, now you go," Sarge says.

"I was sent photos of Harper, and the photos were

covered in fake blood. Pixie was also sent photos of our mother... Care to explain, Killian?"

Killian shrugs. "She was strung out, and a certain someone doesn't like me to murder women if they haven't done anything. When I realized that she was your mom, I sent her with Cal to get clean. Now she is."

"Has anything weird been happening to you?" I ask Enzo, and he shakes his head no.

Enzo's phone rings, halting the conversation. He pulls it from his pocket and holds it to his ear.

"Hello... Okay, we will meet you there." He ends the call, and when he looks at me, I know what he is about to say isn't good.

"Kill, call Cal, and make sure Jordyn's mom is safe. Sarge, take your phone and Pixie's and call the tech guy and offer him double his call-out fee to come now. Doll, we have to meet Kaser at the hospital."

"No," I say, shaking my head. "She won't want to go unless she is dead. Oh my God, is she dead?"

"She won't have to worry about the hospital bill, I will pay whatever her insurance doesn't."

I laugh. "She is a prostitute, Enzo, she doesn't have insurance."

"Don't worry about it, let's just go and see her. Kaser said she is in terrible shape right now."

I nod and follow Enzo, pausing at the door and looking back at Killian. "You better be here when I get back."

He gives me a curt nod, and I continue out the door. Following Enzo into the garage, he opens my door and helps me into Sarge's SUV. I don't question why we are taking this vehicle. It always seems this is the one we travel in most of the time, so I figure it's the safest. I don't speak until we are pulling out of the driveway.

"Why is this happening?"

Enzo puts his hand on my leg. "I have no idea, but I plan to find out. No one threatens my family and gets away with it. If I had to guess, I would say Aldo is playing games with me. We can't find him, and he knows he is dead when we do. He would know what makes everyone weak. Kill's past, Sarge's wife, your sister, and best friend. And me, it's all of you, hurting you hurts me."

The rest of the drive is in silence, and when we park, Enzo waits until someone knocks on his window. Kaser moves back and comes around to my door and opens it. "Harper clearly hates hospitals," he says, pointing to the bruise on his cheek. "She is with a doctor now. I kind of used your husband's name to get them to move faster."

I nod at Kaser and follow Enzo into the emergency room. He goes straight up to the reception, gives her his name and Harper's, and she quickly jumps to her feet and comes to let us in.

"This way, Mr. D'Arco, we have been expecting you."

The lady leads us behind a large double set of doors until she gets to a small cubicle that has the curtains closed.

"If you need anything, please let us know."

Enzo nods, and she leaves us.

"I need you to wait outside."

He looks like he is going to argue, but thankfully, he doesn't. I slide the curtain open a little, and Harper is curled up in a ball on the bed. She doesn't turn to look at who has entered. I walk around the bed and touch her arm; she jumps at the contact.

"Harp, it's me." She moves to look at me, and I gasp as her face comes into view. One of her eyes is swollen shut, and tears stream down her face. I have never seen her cry; she is one of the strongest women I know. I motion for her to scoot over, and I climb up onto the bed. My huge stomach presses against her, and Mars starts to kick up a storm. She places her hand on my stomach, and I wrap mine around her the best that I can.

"There were so many of them. I tried to fight back, but I couldn't. One of them held me down," she sniffles.

"Shh, I'm here now, and they won't hurt you."

We lay in silence while she cries, but nothing I can say or do right now can help how she feels. All I can do is be here when she needs me.

After an hour, a young doctor comes into the cubical and dimly smiles. "Harper, I'm Doctor Stevens, you're free to go. Mr. D'Arco has spoken to the police on your behalf, and all we can do for your injuries is tell you to watch for signs of concussion and take painkillers when needed."

"Thank you," I tell the doctor, who leaves quickly. Enzo steps into the room.

"How is everything going in here? The police will come to the house tomorrow, but I sent them away after the doctor told me you refused a rape kit."

I widen my eyes at him to indicate that he needs to shut up. Of course she didn't want a rape kit. What good would it be? Even if they found the man who did it, she is a prostitute and would be grilled in court over it.

"It's okay, Dolly, he is just trying to help. Let's get out of here before I have to work the next decade to pay off the bill."

"It's been taken care of, you now have insurance. All my employees have medical insurance."

"I don't take handouts, Enzo," Harper snaps, slipping out of the bed.

"And I don't give handouts either. It's a part-time position at my club. It pays well, just like the other dancers, and if you don't dance, you can be a topless waitress or bartender. You can schedule your hours around working at The Range, whatever works best for you. And until I find out who is behind hurting you, you will be coming home with us."

"Okay," she says meekly. I look at her and feel murderous that someone has taken the free spirit of my best friend.

"Can you step out so Harper can get dressed? I have already crash-tackled one naked bitch today."

Enzo smiles at me and steps out from behind the curtain. "I'm going to need to hear that story."

I fill her in on what happened, but I leave out the part about receiving the photos. She doesn't need to worry right now. I will tell her once she has a few days to rest. Once she is dressed, I realize that her dress is ripped and covered in blood. I pop my head out of the curtain, and both Enzo and Kaser are standing side by side.

"I need a jacket."

Kaser slips his arms out of his straight away and hands it to me. Once Harper puts it on, we leave the hospital. I don't know what to say or do. It's totally different when it was her comforting me. She was always the strong one, my rock, and I don't know how to be someone else's rock. It's hard enough being an adult for Pixie.

CHAPTER SEVENTEEN

JORDYN

Once Harper is set up in the privacy of the pool house—I'd rather her be inside with us, but she is used to being on her own and doesn't need us hovering around—I head inside to find Killian. He has some serious explaining to do right now.

Enzo has gone to his office to get updates from Sarge on the phones. Milo is playing Xbox with Pixie and keeping her entertained, so I use the opportunity to go down into the basement. I'm surprised that the main room is empty and even more surprised that the secondary door is ajar. Pushing it open, I follow the hall until I get right to the end and hear a man's voice. My eyes widen as I open the door and find Killian has someone sitting in a chair with wires attached.

"Poppet, you're back. Meet my brother Pike."

"Half-brother," Pike spits, and Killian presses a button on the wall. Pike's body goes rigid, and once Killian lets go of the button, Pike's body relaxes again.

"I'm getting a little concerned about the way you treat

your family." I snort. "First your nephew and now your brother," I say jokingly.

"Payback is a bitch," Killian snaps.

"Fuck you, you're the bitch. I have told you I didn't kill my family, and I have no idea who is trying to kill our sister."

I look between them both as they go back and forth with each other. I can tell this is already going to be exhausting.

"That I already know, and now I know it's someone that's specifically trying to target me, but they don't know me well enough to know killing my family won't hurt my feelings."

I bite at my thumbnail. "Let him go or kill him. We don't have time to fuck around when people are dying. I need to go and see Enzo."

"Let me help," Pike says.

Killian turns around to look at him. "I trusted you once and look how far that got me."

Pike laughs. "Are you seriously holding onto a grudge over something that happened almost two decades ago? We were fucking kids. Our parents were killed, and we were brainwashed into doing whatever the fuck they wanted us to do."

Killian presses the damn green button again. "Aghhhh."

"Okay, now I'm done. I should just kill you, but I do love a good revenge torture. Let me go grab something, and I will let you out."

I wait while Killian leaves the room. My eyes rove over the man, and I can see the resemblance between them. They have the same jawline and eyes.

"So, you tamed my brother?" he asks. "I have kept tabs

on him over the years and honestly thought it was him who killed my family."

I shake my head. "He isn't a complete monster."

Pike laughs. "Then you don't know the real him, he is a monster in every sense of the word."

"He wouldn't murder children, it's not his style. What's your deal, why do you hate your brother?"

"I never hated him. Maybe a little jealous of him and Fiona because they got all the attention. I was a kid when we were taken to that place. It was filled with nightmares, things you couldn't imagine possible. We were no longer siblings. It was every person for themselves, and if we didn't fall in line, awful shit happened. Just look at Killian's face."

"I happen to love his face just the way it is."

Pike smiles just as Killian walks back into the room with a small contraption in his hands. He walks around behind Pike and holds it to his neck, and it makes a clicking sound.

"Fuck," Pike complains, "What the hell was that?"

Killian doesn't answer him straight away, he starts to unclip the arm straps first and then the leg straps before he starts talking.

"It's a very small explosive. If you screw up, all it takes is one text and boom, off with your head." Pike reaches around and feels the back of his neck. "Oh, and don't try to remove it either, it will just blow up if you try."

"Fuck, you're a crazy man."

"Let's go and see Enzo," I say. Both men follow me out of the basement and into Enzo's office.

Enzo raises a brow at Killian as we enter the room.

I sigh, "Enzo, Sarge, meet Killian's brother Pike. Who

now has an explosive in his neck so he doesn't do anything stupid."

"Good to know," Enzo says.

"So, I had a thought. Pike said something downstairs, and it made me think. Everything that's happening with Killian's family, mine, and Sarge isn't a coincidence. I know you said it is Aldo, and that might be true if he just came after my sister and Harper and Sarge, but he didn't know Killian had siblings. So, how would Aldo know if Enzo didn't know? I think it's time to gather Fiona and Cal, and the four of you need to compile a list of who knows you're related. Then we can figure out why they would come after Sarge and I."

"I didn't tell anyone, not even my wife. Not one soul knows from my end."

"Fiona said the only person she told was Ronan, and that was just recently when she went to him for protection."

Enzo's phone vibrates, and he looks down at the caller ID and frowns.

"Why the fuck are you calling me from inside the house?" he snaps. "You're what?"

Enzo places the phone on speaker and rests it on the table.

"Boss, it's not my fault. She slipped past security, and I followed her."

"Where the fuck is my sister, Milo?" I demand. I can't freaking believe this. First, she willingly goes to Lev, and now, she has escaped again.

"Ugh, she wanted to see your mother. I...fuck, she cried and told me what happened to her, and now we are here."

I sigh in relief that she has only gone to see our mother.

From the limited information that Killian has told me about Cal, he is a decent guy.

"So, what's the issue?" Enzo asks.

"I think your ex is banging my dad. I left Pixie to talk with her mom and went to my dad's cabin. She was leaving, but he stepped out in his boxers."

"Thanks, Milo, just stay with my sister and bring her home when she is done. We will handle this."

I end the call, and Enzo starts pacing the room. "Do you think Cat is behind all of this?" Sarge asks.

"Cat, Cal, I'm going to fucking kill them both!" Enzo shouts.

"Cal wouldn't, I know him better than anyone."

Enzo turns to face Killian. "How can you be so fucking sure? He knows about your siblings, and he has Jordyn's mother with him, so he could know how close Jordyn and Harper are. All the pieces are fitting together right now."

Killian's confidence doesn't waiver; his body language shows how sure he is. I can't lie, it all seems like Cal and Cat are behind this, but why? If it was just Cat being jealous of me, there are better ways she could get back at me. She has no beef with Killian or even Sarge.

"Let's all calm down and come up with a plan. Kill, you call Cal and get him here, Enzo, you call Cat, she will come running if she thinks she has a chance with you. Jordyn, you go and spend the rest of the day with Harper. I will call Milo and make sure he keeps Pixie out of the house all day. And you," Sarge says, looking at Pike, "Kill can deal with you."

No one argues with Sarge, and I can see why he makes a good right-hand man for Enzo. All three of my men surround me.

"We will be in and out all day, so stay in the pool house with Harper, and Kaser will be standing at the door all day. No one comes in or out unless it's us," Enzo says. I open my mouth, but Killian steps up close behind me, his hand covering my mouth.

"Don't argue with him, Poppet. We have some killin' to do, and I can't be worrying about you." All I can do is nod, and he removes his hand. "Good girl, now go keep our baby safe."

"Our baby," I whisper.

Sarge steps in closer next to Enzo so that they are shoulder to shoulder. "Our baby. He might be Enzo's DNA, but we are a family. You, me, Enzo, Kill, Pixie, and Mars."

Tears prickle my eyes. A family. All I have ever wanted was a proper family. Nodding again is all I can do because the lump in my throat restricts my voice. Enzo cups my face and leans down. "We need you in our lives, Doll. You have given me things I have always wanted."

He presses his lips to mine, his tongue sweeps inside my mouth. When he pulls back, he leaves me breathless.

Sarge pulls me to him, and Enzo willingly steps back. "Thank you for staying behind. I can't lose you."

He places his forehead against mine, and his mismatched eyes say the words that he can't; what happened to Missy has broken a part of him that can't ever be fixed. He needs to know I'm safe and that he won't lose me. "I promise I won't leave."

"If you are a good girl for us, I promise to tie you to the bed tonight, and you will have all our hands all over you."

A shiver runs through my body, and Killian chuckles. "Can we go, you're all making me want to gag," Pike says.

"Tick, tick, boom, brother. Have some patience if you like your head attached to your body."

Pike laughs. "You do realize that I just lost my wife and children, and when we find the fuckers that killed them, I expect you to detonate."

Sarge and Pike share a look, one of understanding. "I'll do it," Sarge says, and Pike nods at him.

"Go before this starts getting too morbid. I'm going to check on Harper," I say, and I'm the first to leave Enzo's office and head to the pool house. Kaser follows me outside and watches as I walk inside the pool house.

"Harp," I call out when she isn't in the open living room area. I check the bedroom and hear the shower running. I cross the bedroom and push the door open. "Harp."

She still doesn't answer me. I rush to the shower and pull the steamed door open. She sits on the floor with the water beating down on her and a razor blade between her fingers. "Shit."

I quickly step in and lean forward to turn the water off. The heat is turned up so high, it burns my skin.

"I can't make it go away. I need it to leave my brain, Jordyn, I need it to go away."

Squatting down, I sit beside her and pull her into my arms. "It doesn't feel like it, but it will be okay. I promise."

She nods her head. I don't know what her healing journey will look like, everyone is different, but one thing I know is I won't let her be a victim. Harper Lou Daniels will be a survivor.

"You're the strongest person I know. Go easy on yourself, you're allowed to be angry, sad, and angry again. It isn't fair what happened."

"I hate feeling weak," she cries. "I don't know if I can go back there."

Wiping the hair from her face behind her ears, I murmur, "Then don't. Enzo has given you a job, and I'm sure he will make it full-time if that's what you want. Plus, you are welcome to stay in the pool house as long as you want. I vote forever since I'm having a freaking baby, me, and I have no idea how to be a good mother."

Harper chuckles. "You will be the best mom, just like you were to Pixie."

I sigh. "I don't know how good I did with her. She was taken into sex trafficking. Then she helped someone escape and wanted to stay with him, and now she has run off to see our mother, who is now clean and living in some off-the-grid community."

"We are both a mess," she says, and we both laugh. Harper untangles herself from my arms and stands, offering me her hand. She pulls me to my feet and gasps.

"When was the last time you shaved your legs, woman? How do you have three fine men when you look like Bigfoot?"

"Excuse me," I laugh. "The rule is, if I can't see it or reach it, I can't shave it."

"Then it's sorted, we are fixing that. I need to take my mind off everything, and you need me right now."

"I doubt we have any wax here, and we can't leave right now."

"It's fine, I can make some."

Harper walks out of the room, and I follow behind her. "Harp, you're naked."

She smiles at me, goes back into her room, and comes

back out in sweats and a crop tee that hangs just under her breasts, her toned stomach on display. She marches to the door, and Kaser is standing there with a younger man.

"Kip, I need some supplies. I need a bag of sugar, some lemons, and a saucepan."

The young guy nods and looks at Kaser.

"Go," Kaser says. "Get the lady what she needs."

I wish I knew in advance how much pain I was about to be in by the time she was done. Killian and his blade were a walk in the park in comparison.

CHAPTER EIGHTEEN

ENZO

Cat agreed to meet me, and it pains me to know I have to be nice to the woman who is actively trying to ruin my relationship. I always knew Cat was a certain kind of woman, and once upon a time, I thought she would make a great wife to have by my side. I'm glad that she screwed my brother, and I got to see the real her. Some might say it's no different from Jordyn being with Sarge and Killian, but the difference is, I want them with her.

Sarge walks into my office, and I have to admit, it's strange seeing him dressed down every day. But it does suit him. "Milo will entertain Pixie until dinner time and keep me updated. What else would you like me to do?"

Standing from my chair, I close the distance between us and take his hands in mine. "Just relax, everything will be fine."

He nods. "I want to believe that, but I have this gnawing feeling in my stomach that something is going to happen."

"Nothing is going to happen." I shake my head. "We

have all the bases covered, and I have men everywhere. No one is getting in or out without us knowing. Killian will bring Cal in, Cat is on her way, and Jordyn is in the pool house with Harper. We will get answers today and deal with it."

"What is this between us, Enzo? I hate not knowing. With Jordyn, I know where I stand, but us..."

"You're mine as much as Jordyn is ours. Things will settle down soon, and I will show you how I feel. That you're mine."

The asshole snorts. "For as long as I have known you, showing your feelings has not been your strong suit."

"A man can change, can't he? Maybe being in love has changed me."

His eyes widen. "In love?"

I shrug. "Yeah, I think so. I don't know how it happened, but the thought of anyone hurting her makes me murderous. I miss her when she isn't around, and my heart does backflips every time she is in the room. I didn't feel any of that with Cat."

"And what about me?"

I smile up at him and lick my lips. "You're my best friend. I couldn't imagine not having you in my life..."

"And you like my cock."

I bellow out a laugh. "That too."

My phone alerts me that someone is at the gate. I check it and accept the request for security to let Cat in.

"Cat is here. Could you call my father and brother and fill them in? Tell Angelo to be on standby in case I need him. Now kiss me so I have your taste on my tongue to save me from gagging when I have to be nice to Cat."

Sarge takes my chin in his hand before his lips smash to

mine. He dominates my space; his light citrus smell surrounds us. I want nothing more than to let him take me right here so Cat can see how much I don't want her, but that won't help me.

When he sucks my bottom lip into his mouth, his free hand runs over the length of my dick. His touch makes me moan. Fuck! I want him so badly it hurts.

"That will give you something to think about while you deal with the leech. Have fun with that, by the way."

He winks at me and leaves. I tuck my cock up, I don't want it to look like a damn tent in my pants when Cat walks in.

Speaking of, she struts into my office in a tight red dress that doesn't leave a lot to the imagination.

"You summoned me?" she asks.

"I wanted to apologize; I made a mistake."

Cat laughs. "Cut the shit, Enzo. I have known you a long fucking time, and you don't apologize, and you certainly never admit to making a mistake."

"You caught me," I say, reaching down to open my desk drawer and pulling out my personal gun, one reserved for family or friends. "Do you know what happens when you go against the family?"

"Of course I do, but I don't think you understand what happens when you cross me."

She keeps talking as I raise my weapon. "I have been doing my research, Enzo, and it really isn't that hard when you know where to look. I'm surprised you have caught on so quickly. They were all supposed to be dead first. I wanted them to see it coming. That whore surviving the attack was a shame."

"You didn't count on being seen with Cal, but you see, your mistake was going after Kill's family members, ones he doesn't care about."

"Maybe," she shrugs, "But I didn't want any loose ends after I killed him. I kind of hoped one of them would have done it for me because, you know, opening old wounds can do that. I wanted to show you he lied to you for all these years."

I laugh at how crazy she sounds. "He doesn't owe me the truth; he owes me his loyalty."

She scoffs. "A man who won't take the oath to be part of your 'family.'"

Her air quotes piss me off. "So, what was your endgame, Cat?"

"You. It was always supposed to be us. I was going to frame everything on the Russians, but the idiots gave you back the girl. Fucking weak. Cal was my next scapegoat, but I guess the cat is out of the bag now."

"Just know I won't take any pleasure from killing you."

She smiles, walks over to the office window, and stares out of it for a second. "I wouldn't do that if I were you."

"And why not? You had to know it was going to happen."

She shrugs. "I did, but if I can't have you, Enzo, no one can. Including her."

"What did you do?" I shout, unable to control my temper.

She fucking cackles, and when she doesn't answer me, I fire a warning shot, and the window shatters.

"Your men guarding her are probably dead right now."

Dread fills me just as Sarge busts through the door. "Go

check on Jordyn now!" He doesn't wait for me; he turns and runs. "If you so much as hurt her."

She steps back from the window. "You'll what, Enzo, kill me? I already know that, but you will have to live out the rest of your life knowing I took her from you."

I need to do something. "The baby, Cat. You think I care all that much about a whore I married to make you jealous? No. Mars is the heir to my fucking empire."

"If you don't kill me, I can bring you the baby. Cutting him out can be easily done."

I pace back and forth across the room. Fuck, I need my father, he will know what to do. "Did your father get the present I left him yet?"

How the fuck did she read my mind? Pulling my phone from my pocket, I dial his number. "Son, Sarge called me. Is everything okay?"

"Just peachy."

What Cat doesn't know is that me and my father have always had code words. Just peachy is code for I'm in serious trouble.

"Have you had any deliveries today?"

He says that he hasn't, but he will send Giovanni to go and check the gate.

"Let me know once he is back."

"I will, and I know you can't say anything, so just reply yes if I am close."

I look up at Cat, and she just watches me. "Is the person with you right now?"

"Yes, make Giovanni hurry up, the suspense is killing me."

"Is it Cat, because Sarge told me she was on her way?"

"Sure is."

My father sighs. "I'm so sorry, son. I haven't been truthful since I have been back. She was involved in helping your mother make me disappear, but she doesn't know that I know. I have been having her followed. I wanted to see who else she is working with...Oh, fuck."

"Dad, what?"

"We will be there soon."

My father ends the call, and I shove my phone into my pocket. I can't just stand here and look at this bitch anymore; she isn't going to tell me where Jordyn is. Hopefully, Killian can get some answers out of her.

"You know what?" I say to her. "You win." This makes her stand taller and smile. "I should have picked you, but my mother wanted it so badly that it put me off. She always did that."

"We could still be good together, me, you, and even the baby. Though, we would need to rethink the name Mars."

I close the distance between us. I don't take joy in hurting women, but she has left me with no choice. She must realize her mistake of letting her guard down when I bring the butt of my gun down on her head. She slumps to the floor like a sack of potatoes. Tucking the gun away, I drag her toward the door—the carpet makes it hard, and I have to pick her up and throw her over my shoulder.

Not wasting any time, I take her to the basement and quickly chain her up before racing back upstairs and out to the pool hall. My men have swarmed the area, and my heart beats erratically until I hear Sarge barking orders. All the dead men are to be moved into the freezer in the basement. Kill is a crazy asshole who has a whole walk-in freezer.

Kaser is lying on the ground while Sarge holds something over his stomach. "I will be fine."

"You have been fucking shot, idiot. The ambulance will be here soon. You know the go-to story, and the paramedics are on our payroll."

"Fine, send someone who can sketch to the hospital. I saw the asshole's face."

"Fuck! Everyone get back to your posts now, and someone get more men here. I want to double down on security again."

Honking at the gates catches my attention, and I pull my weapon and go around to the front of the house as both my father's and Killian's cars pull into the driveway.

Running to Kill's car, he steps out. "What the fuck is going on?" he asks.

"Jordyn and Harper are gone, Cat fucking blindsided me. I have her in the basement."

Kill nods. "Pike, get Cal down to the basement, chain him up somewhere. I will be down shortly."

My father steps out of his car along with his brothers. "You need to see this."

Both Kill and I round the car and look in the boot that Giovanni pops open. Inside is Aldo, dead as fuck.

"What am I looking at besides a dead rat?" I ask, and my father lifts Aldo's shirt. There is a symbol carved into his chest.

"I know what that is," Kill says. He doesn't elaborate; he runs to his car and puts it in reverse before peeling out of the driveway.

Sarge comes to my side and interlocks our fingers. "I should have listened to you."

"Not even I would have predicted this," Sarge says, squeezing my hand.

CHAPTER NINETEEN

KILLIAN

That stupid fucking bitch played me, but she doesn't know I have been following her for years. It might be far and few between jobs, but she always leaves a calling card. The rune for feminine strength carved into the chest of her male victims.

Pulling into the driveway of Ronan's estate, his security stops me, and if I wasn't so dead set on not starting a war with them, I would have driven straight through the fucking thing.

"Name," the man states, and I roll my eyes as if the fucker doesn't know who I am.

"Killian Masters."

The pudgy man's eyes go wide as a dinner plate. He scrambles back into his little box, picks up a handset, and calls through to the house. Within seconds, the gate opens, and I drive up the obnoxiously long driveway. Ronan and Darragh meet me outside, both men stand side by side with their arms crossed over their chests.

I stop mere inches from Ronan, and he doesn't budge an inch, he just smirks at me. Getting out of the car, I slam the door.

"Kill, what can I do for you?" he asks in his stupid accent that makes me want to punch him in the throat.

"Where the fuck is my sister? I need her location."

Darragh laughs as if I was trying to be funny. "We can't tell you that, then you would know the location of our safe house."

I scoff. "If you don't tell me, I will find every house you own, murder every person inside, and burn them to the ground, and it will be the start of a war so fucking big your grandchildren won't be safe from me."

Darragh tries to step forward, but Ronan throws his arm out to stop him.

"Come inside so we can talk about what is going on, and I will decide if I can help you."

I nod, and Darragh leads the way inside with an attitude that could very well put him on my shit list.

Inside, we are not alone, Cian and Sullivan are in the living room.

"Sit," Ronan demands. "We have our own issues to deal with right now, so if you could make this quick."

"How quick is this for you? My sister double-crossed me, for what reason I have no idea yet, but she killed Enzo's father's right-hand man."

"The one who was working against your father? Sounds to me like she did you a favor," Darragh says. I cut a glare at him.

"That isn't the issue, good riddance. The issue is she is

working with the bitch who just had my woman kidnapped, along with her best friend, Harper."

Cian jumps to his feet. "Why the fuck didn't you lead with that?! Our Angel is in trouble!"

My phone starts buzzing in my palm. I open the message from Sarge, and an image pops up on my screen. It's the men who took them.

I turn my phone. "You all don't happen to know who the fuck these dead men are?"

"Shit," Ronan swears under his breath. "They're our men, but you have my word that we had no idea. We will give you the location of our safe house, but we are coming with you."

"I want her alive, I will have fun tearing her apart." I seethe.

Ronan nods. "We want Harper."

Fuck, I can't trade Poppet's best friend for the location, can I? Shit. Something tells me they will come for her no matter what I agree to. Trying to have a moral compass for her benefit is fucking hard.

"Fine, but you don't lay a finger on my woman if she tries to fight you on it."

Sullivan laughs. "You really think we would hurt a pregnant bitch? Jesus, our reputation really has gone to shit."

I should call Sarge and Enzo and let them come with us, but that is only wasting more time. They can hate me later when I tell them. Time is ticking, and I won't waste any when it comes to Jordyn.

"You can follow us." Ronan says.

"You might want to bring some weapons; you have no

idea how lethal Fiona is. We all had to kill to survive. She is quick and precise."

Once they have gathered their weapons, they all head out to their SUV. I get into my car and follow them, hoping like hell we find Jordyn at the safe house. I can't imagine my sister being that stupid, but it really depends on what Cat's endgame is.

My ringtone for Sarge blares through the car, and I hit answer.

"Where the fuck are you? We need answers from Cat and Cal. They took Jordyn, Kill."

Keeping my eyes trained on the car in front of me so I don't lose them, because they are driving like a fucking maniac. "I have a better lead that could find Jordyn. Send Pike down to start making them talk; just stay with him and make sure he doesn't kill them. We might need more specific answers when I get back. Tell Enzo to separate Cal and Cat; he might be able to talk to Cat and manipulate her. I will be back as soon as I can."

Sarge sighs. "Do what needs to be done but Kill…I can't lose her, I won't survive it."

"You know me, I will do what needs to be done. Start locating their family members and get a team with eyes on them. Don't tell Enzo or Mario about that part, he might not agree to me hurting close family friends, but I will slaughter them all in front of everyone if I have to."

"Done," he says. I expected him to put up more of a fight, but when you bring in threats to hurt people close to them, they generally start talking, and if anyone can rival me in technique, it's Pike. I learned a lot of what I know from him, even if he was a traitor and did a lot of the torture on us like the good little sheep he was.

My perception of time sucks. We could have been driving for half an hour or twelve hours, and I wouldn't know, but when they pull over, I bring my car to a stop behind him and get out, heading for the driver's side window. Darragh rolls it down.

"Get in, if we bring your shit box of a car in, she will know something is up. If it's just Ronan's car, she might think he is just checking up on her."

"Doubtful. If she was expecting the body drop today, she is probably gone."

Stepping back, the back passenger door opens, and I slip inside. "I have cameras in the house, she is still there. But my men are missing. Which I expected. She has left herself open by sending them to do her dirty work."

Darragh moves forward, and I watch out the window to see what surrounds the property. It's deserted, which you would expect from a safe house. If she even tried to run, she would get lost, which works for me. I would happily let her die and be eaten by wild animals.

We pull into a driveway, and the only way to tell is the letter box and the gap between the trees. When the SUV comes to a stop, two pigtailed girls throw the door open and squeal.

"Fuck, I hate kids," Ronan snaps but quickly plasters a smile on his face and steps out of the car with his arms open wide.

I slip from the car. "Keep the children entertained, they seem to like you. Everyone else, be ready. If she has a sniper rifle, we are fucked."

I take one step, and a bullet flies right past my head. I spoke too soon. "Get the girls in the car, Ronan."

"Sister, we need to have a talk. You don't want me to kill your children, do you?" I yell so she can hear me wherever she is.

I walk closer to the house, and Darragh stands by my side. "I would listen to the man."

"What's stopping me from ending all of you and taking the children?" Fiona asks. We both look up and see her on the roof of the house.

"The fact that Ronan hates children, and I made him a deal to give me your location. If he ends one twin, imagine how scared the other would be before her death. One would have to see it coming."

"You wouldn't dare," she snaps.

I walk closer. "You have my woman, Fiona. I would kill anyone who gets in the way."

I'm talking shit out of my ass; I don't think even I could kill innocent children, but she doesn't know that.

The front door slightly moves. "Get down!" I yell, and we all drop as the man steps outside and sprays bullets.

"Kill the children!" someone yells, and the man drops to the ground. Fiona just put a bullet in his brain.

"Fine, you win. Just don't hurt them. I'm coming down."

"What's the plan now?" Cian asks.

"We search the house and make sure Jordyn and Harper are not here, then I'll take Fiona to Enzo's. I will call Enzo and let him know we are coming."

Fiona steps out from the house, her hands in the air. Sullivan hands me some handcuffs and cable ties.

Tears run down my sister's face. "Please don't hurt the girls. They were supposed to be in the safe room."

"You should have known I would come for you after leaving your calling card."

Fiona gasps. "She dropped the body already? That fucking bitch double-crossed me."

She doesn't resist being put in cuffs. Sullivan stays with her, and I tell him to not let her in the car with her children. Cian, Darragh, and I go inside to search for the girls, but I'm confident that they're not here if the security is not here.

After a thorough walkthrough, they are definitely not here. We head back outside, and luckily, my sister is where we left her. I grasp her by the back of the hair and make her stand. "Where the fuck is Jordyn?"

"I don't know. She was supposed to take them tomorrow night, and we were going to leave. I didn't care what she did to her."

"Why, why the fuck would you come for her, the one good thing in my life? I spared yours."

"You were supposed to die, you're a danger to anyone close to you. No one wanted you, it's why our parents ran. It's your fault. You killed her; you killed our cousin."

My brows furrow. "What the fuck are you talking about?"

Darragh pulls out his gun and aims it at me. "You killed Connor?"

I shake my head. "Seriously, I was fucking four when we ran. I didn't kill anyone, so try again, sis."

She shrugs and laughs. "Was worth a try on the chance they shot first and asked questions later."

"Your parents ran because your father was a rat, and

your mother was a traitor for leaving with him. They went to their graves, not telling a soul where you were, and once you were found, my father sent you to that place as a punishment for your parents' sins."

"This is all great reminiscing about the past, but how the fuck is it all tied to Enzo?"

Fiona sighs. "Because I had a job to kill Enzo, and guess who popped up and ruined it all? My own fucking brother. Then you had to be you and get all extra and rip my boss's little brother's throat out. Then Jordyn popped up, and Cat seemed like a perfect target to use to get to you and kill you. Little did I know the stupid bitch had her own plan, and all she has done is make everything go to shit."

"As fun as this is, I should kill you now, but I think our brother wants to have a little chat with you about why his family is dead."

Panic flits across her eyes. "No, not him, please, Killian."

"We are wasting time, let's get back to Enzo's," Ronan says, and I nod.

"Here is what is going to happen. You will get in the car and do not alert the girls that anything is happening. Then we will take my car to Enzo's."

Fiona nods. "Please make sure they are looked after; they are just children. I saved them just like someone should have saved me."

"They're not even yours?"

She nods her head yes. "I just didn't tell Darragh he was their father."

Well fuck, that information isn't going to go down well when he finds out. Maybe I won't have to be the one to kill my sister after all.

CHAPTER TWENTY

SARGE

Killian has been gone for hours, and watching Pike makes my stomach churn. He has left Cat isolated and in the dark. He seems to think with her being so vain, having her hear what's happening, but taking away her vision will help scare her into talking once Kill gets back.

"What did you tell her, Cal?"

"Nothing," he says, and Pike hits the contraption in his hand, and the clamps on his nipples spark to life, sending jolts of electricity into him.

"Then how the fuck did she know about me or Fiona? You are the only common denominator."

The door to the basement slams open, and Kill comes down the stairs with a woman thrown over his shoulder.

"About fucking time," I snap, pushing to my feet.

"I brought you a present," Kill says to Pike. "She might have some insight into your family being killed. She was working with Cat, but it seems Cat has outsmarted her."

"She didn't outsmart me, she framed me, wanting me to take the fall for everything."

Pike steps closer to his sister, wrapping his hand around her throat. "You killed my wife and children."

"Fuck you. Does it hurt deep down inside knowing they are gone? You watched those pigs rape me and did nothing. You both deserve to die."

"Did my ten-year-old son deserve to die or my six-year-old daughter?"

He loosens his grip on her neck. "No, they were not supposed to, but they came downstairs. I couldn't let them live a life after seeing their mother die, so I put them out of their misery. This is your fault. Growing up with you as a parent would have ruined them."

Pike laughs, and fuck, it's disturbing. "You don't fucking know me anymore, and maybe once I kill you, I will raise those little girls just to spite you."

"No," Fiona says, "please no."

Pike drags her away through the set of doors that leads to other rooms. Kill helps Cal down from the chain.

Cal slaps his hands away once he is able to use his hands. "Fuck you. Did you really think I would spill your secrets?"

"I don't know, brother; you were fucking the woman who orchestrated the woman I love to be kidnapped."

"The woman that we love," Enzo says, coming down the stairs. "Ronan has Fiona's phone and has made contact with her security; she has informed them of a change of plans and that Cat has picked her up. We just need to talk to Cat and find out where the men are hiding out. When we asked about a location, they needed confirmation from both Fiona and Cat."

"It's smart, really," I say.

"It's not," Kill adds. "They have just been alerted. Cat had double-crossed Fiona, but she didn't know the location, and I don't think she ever did."

"Get her out. It's time we showed her what happens when you double-cross me," Enzo says. I walk over to a large double-door closet. It is where Kill keeps his chemicals. Pike made me shove her in there with them. It was a tight fit, but I managed. Opening the doors, she falls out.

"Enzo! Get Enzo for me!" she cries.

Enzo steps forward and starts to clap. Cat looks up at him, "You know," he says, squatting down beside her. "I can no longer save you, Cat, because I can't trust you. My father told me that you were working with my mother, and now you have orchestrated all of this. Do the right thing for once before you die."

"Fuck you, Enzo, I would have made the perfect wife. Me!"

Enzo laughs and takes her chin. "I never wanted to marry you; it was a relief when Angelo fucked you. But make no mistake, you will be kept alive until I find Jordyn, so she can kill you herself. We know who has her. One thing you didn't consider was the idiots took Harper, and the Irish have a thing for her. They are scouring the streets as we talk, and someone, somewhere, will have seen them."

A knock at the side door makes everyone freeze and stare. No one comes to that door, ever, or at least we have never seen anyone besides Cal use that entrance. Kill casually walks to the door and throws the door open.

"Just in time," he says as two of our soldiers step through the door, dragging in Cat's younger brother. The kid isn't cut out for this life. She has always protected him; he lives in a college dorm and is bright as fuck.

Cat screams when Enzo forces her to look at her brother. I know Enzo must be pissed off right now, but he doesn't show it.

"Take him through the back and second door on the right. We might start with some light electrocution. I like it when they cry," Kill says with a half laugh, half morbid chuckle. Fuck, the crazy bastard scares me sometimes. "Sarge, grab the bitch; she will want to watch this."

I get closer to her and lean down, grabbing her bicep, and pulling her to her feet. "This could all be over if you just tell us where she is. You know Kill will just work his way through your family members until there are none left, and only you have the power to stop this."

She shakes her head no, and I force her to follow behind her brother as Kill takes him to his fucked-up electricity room.

Cat watches on as Kill straps her brother into the chair. "I'm so sorry. I love you, but if I tell him where she is, it will have all been for nothing."

"Did you ever love Enzo at all? Cat, you sound like a spoiled little girl throwing a tantrum, and you're willing to risk your brother. You do realize how much pain you're in for, right? Kill knows how to bring you to the brink of death, begging for it all to end, just to bring you back, over and over again."

"If it gets rid of that whore from his life, I will do whatever it takes."

I push the bitch toward Kill and storm out of the room. I have never wanted to lay hands on a woman, and she sure as hell won't make me go against everything I believe in.

I don't stop when Enzo calls my name. I go back upstairs and hope that our tech wiz can help with facial recognition. Someone has to have seen something.

CHAPTER TWENTY-ONE

JORDYN

The room is dark, and no matter where you look, you can't see very far in front of you. If I hold my arm all the way out, it's lost in the darkness. Harper cuddles up to my side, and for a woman who has just been through what she has, she sure put up one hell of a fight when two men stormed into the pool house.

The right side of her face is swollen from where she was hit. She latched on to one of them so hard, the asshole will have scars from her nails on his face. From what we can tell, we are in a basement, with one small window. We have to have been here for a few days if the routine is anything to go by. The men come down and bring us sandwiches and water, and the stench from the bucket in the corner of the room where we relieve ourselves isn't nice.

"Do you think they will find us?" Harper asks while squeezing my hand.

"I have no doubt that they will."

I don't add as long as they don't come down here and kill

us first, which is an option. It's always an option. I have seen firsthand what Killian does.

"What I don't understand is why those men look familiar... I swear I have seen the beefy one before. What if it's the same men..."

I take in a deep breath. "Harp, those men were there for me, and what happened to you was because of me. Enzo might kill me for telling you this, but we have all been targeted, me, Sarge, and Killian, and we think it might be Cat."

Harper gasps. "The ex? That's fucked up. Does Enzo have a magic cock or something?"

I snort. Of course my best friend is trying to make light of the situation. She should yell at me, blame me for what happened to her.

"Or something. But why are you not mad at me? Those men hurt you because you are friends with me."

"You're my ride or die, Dolly. You didn't send them in to hurt me. Someone else is responsible for that. Now, we need to stop waiting around like sitting ducks and see if we can find some weapons. Those men will be back, and I don't plan to die here."

Harper stands and offers me her hand that I can barely see, even though my eyes have adjusted slightly to the darkness. It must be late at night to offer no light through the window.

"Harp," I say as I stand, and a warmth trickles down my leg.

"Yeah?"

Tears fill my eyes. "I think I pissed my pants."

When I sniffle, she giggles. "Don't worry about it, you do

know what I do for a living. Just last month, some guy paid me to pee on him. Easiest five hundred bucks I've ever made."

We move around the room and find what we can, anything to protect ourselves. With each step, I feel wetter, if that is even possible.

"I don't think it's pee."

Her silhouette moves, and she places her hands on my shoulders. "Okay, you're pregnant. I have seen movies. Is it blood? Oh, are you far enough that your water could have broken?"

At the mention of blood, I move my hand under my panties and run my fingers over the wetness. When I pull them out and try to see, it's no use.

"You need to taste it," Harper says.

"What the fuck! No, I am not licking my fingers right now. We should be able to smell blood." I lift my fingers to my nose, and it doesn't smell like blood. "I don't think that it's blood."

"Fuck it, I will taste it to be sure. Enzo can owe me big time."

I snort and pull my hand away. There is no way she is tasting it, either. "No matter what it is, Harper, we can't do anything right now."

Harper starts to pace and mumbles to herself. I try to follow her with my eyes until I hear the sound of glass smashing.

"Harper, what are you doing? They will come down here."

"Good," she says. "Hopefully, they turn the lights on.

We have sat and waited long enough. We have to do something."

The sound of boots above us is loud as they stomp across the floor. Harper pushes me back until my back is flat against a wall. "Stay there, and if they flick the light on, check for blood. Just don't worry about me. We need to get you out of here."

I nod even though I doubt that she can see me. The boots get closer as they come down a set of stairs, and the jingle of keys has my heart beating erratically.

The door opens, and light filters in. "What the fuck are you bitches doing?"

The man steps into the room, and his eyes land on me with my hand once more down my pants, pulling them out so I can see what's going on.

A shrill scream fills the room, and I see Harper running toward the man. He smirks at her, but I don't think he expects her to have something in her hand. She launches her body at him, and I watch in horror as her body goes flying across the room, but the man clutches the front of his throat. Looking back to Harper, she groans but pulls herself to her feet. A second man comes running down the stairs, and this time, she has a small iron bar. He closes in on her, grabs her by her hair, and forces her onto her tippy toes as the third man rushes in and tries to help the man that has fallen to the floor. The idiots rip the large shard of glass from his throat, and blood sprays everywhere. The girliest shriek comes from one of the men, causing him to pass out.

"Fuck," the third says, letting Harper go and running over to the man with blood squirting from him, placing his hand over his wound. Harper picks up a lump of fucking wood and sneaks closer, swinging it. The thunk is stomach-churning but exciting as he slumps over the other man.

"Dolly, it's time to fucking run now."

We both run toward the door. I'm the first out, and Harper follows behind. She gets halfway up the stairs before she turns back. I stop and watch in horror. Why would she go back? Relief washes over me as she pulls the door shut and slides the latch in place. It's not locked, but it's enough that we can make our escape.

Once we are upstairs, Harper puts her finger over her lips, and we tiptoe through the house. Just because there were only three men when they brought us here doesn't mean there isn't anyone else here.

"Do you think anyone else is here?" I whisper, and she shrugs. We walk through the kitchen, and Harper holds up a set of keys and nods toward the door. Once we successfully make it outside, I look around, and if I'm not mistaken, we are in Huntersville—the somewhat nicer part where people own or rent houses and don't live in shitty apartments.

"Harp, did that seem a little too easy?"

Harper scoffs. "Bitch please, I think that asshole broke my ribs. But babe, I couldn't just sit around anymore. So, get in the fucking car already."

She presses a buzzer and one of the two cars' lights flash; I waddle towards the car, and I'm hit with a pressure in my stomach that winds me. "Harp, something doesn't feel right."

She rushes toward me and helps me into the car. Thank fuck it's low to the ground, or I wouldn't be able to get in.

She closes the door once I'm in, and I lock the door, not taking any chances. I check to make sure that it's not blood, and when my hand comes up clean, I sigh in relief. At least we will have time to get home, so the guys stop worrying.

When Harper doesn't get in straight away, I try to see what she is doing. Time keeps ticking by, and she jumps into the car and laughs.

"I used the key to let the air out of the tires. I didn't want to chance one waking...Oh fuck," she says, putting the keys in the ignition. A really big man is standing in the doorway. She turns the car over, and fuck, it's a stick shift; she curses. I know she can't drive one for shit, never has been able to.

The man gets closer to the car. "Harp, don't overthink this, just remember what you were taught."

She starts talking through the steps out loud, and before we know it, we are reversing. When she stops and gets the car to go forward, a menacing grin takes over her whole fucking face. I look from her to the man, and he must realize what is about to happen. Harper heads straight toward him, grinding gears, but she hits the man and slams on the brakes.

"This wasn't as bad as I remember," she says with a giggle, putting the car back in reverse. Fuck. We just ran him over a second time. "Hopefully he is dead."

Another pang of pain hits me, and I grip the oh fuck handle. Harper doesn't try and run the man down again, she turns the car around and drives out onto the road. We start to approach a red light, even though the road is deserted.

"Harper, slow the fuck down."

"I CAN'T! I haven't mastered stopping without stalling. Hold on. We need to get you home to your men."

I nod, holding on for dear life. The light on the clock that is on the dash says it's almost midnight. No wonder the roads are dead.

"I fucking love you, Jordyn Rae D'Arco."

I smile at the sound of my new name. "I fucking love you too, Harper Lou Daniels. Now let's go home, so my husband can take my ass to the hospital."

"Shit, should we go there first?"

I shake my head no. From what I have read, I have twenty-four hours to have this baby if it is my water that has broken. The pains are low, and since sitting, I haven't had another one. He just kicked, which means he is moving.

"No, Enzo might have kittens if we go to the hospital in Huntersville."

Harper nods and keeps her eyes on the road. Tears well in my eyes as I watch her. My best friend is fierce, and I don't know where she just found the strength to take down those men, but I will be forever grateful that she did.

CHAPTER TWENTY-TWO

PIXIE

I'm sick of being kept in the dark. I know something is happening, and that Milo is just keeping me busy. As soon as we got home, I was rushed upstairs, and Milo wouldn't let me leave the room. He even went as far as to tell me that the dickhead ordered us to stay up here.

Milo passed out ten minutes ago, and I have been waiting patiently to sneak downstairs and see what the fuck is going on.

I loved staying with Lev, he didn't treat me like a child. But he thinks he can send me away because I need to be with my family. I know he was right about that, but he thinks his life isn't for a child, again with that word. I'm almost thirteen, and I will show him I am worthy. He told me I deserve vengeance for what those men did to me, but he tells me I should bide my time, learn how to defend myself, and how to kill a man, and Killian is the man who can teach me just that.

I sneak past Milo, slip out the door, and tip-toe downstairs. The entire house seems eerily quiet. Where the hell is everyone? Jordyn wasn't in Enzo's room; Sarge's bed doesn't look like he has slept in it. Kill is always home, he hates leaving the basement, even though he has banned me from ever stepping foot in there again after letting Lev out. He needs to understand Lev was the only good thing about my time away, the men who would come and go didn't give a shit how they hurt me. But Lev... he would bring me clean clothes and food. He told me that my tears wouldn't help me, I needed to be strong, and he was right, those men wanted my tears.

"Kill!" I shout as I descend the basement stairs, announcing myself. I would hate to sneak up on the guy. "Kill, I'm coming down the stairs. I'm almost at the door, speak now or forever hold your peas or whatever that saying is."

Popping my head through the door, there is no sign of Kill, but Cat is hanging from the ceiling. I wonder what she did to royally fuck up.

"Pix, thank God. I need you to let me down."

Walking closer to her, she watches me, begging me with her eyes. I wish I could help her, but I'm no idiot. If a woman is tied up down here, she has done something terrible.

Shrill screams come from the hallway. Ignoring Cat, I walk to the door and press my ear to it.

"Yes, go in there and save my brother. They are crazy, Pix; they think I hurt Jordyn, and I would never do that."

"Wouldn't you?" I ask, keeping my ear to the door. "Is Kill in there?"

"Nope, they all left, his brother is, though."

That makes my ears perk up. "Kill has a brother, who knew."

"I can't say I'm surprised to see you here; I have been listening to everyone talk and piecing together what you're doing. It's smart really, and I could learn a thing or two from you. Kill's family, I get, but why Sarge and Missy?"

Cat laughs. "I wanted him to spiral, paying someone to go back on social media and get her voiceprint wasn't hard. If his mind was elsewhere, it would have been easier to get to Jordyn. With her gone, Sarge would have offed himself, Fiona, the useless bitch, was supposed to kill her brother, but she had her own agenda, so I had to take care of her."

"Such an elaborate plan just to be with the dickhead, if you ask me. Let's circle back to the fact that Kill has a brother, is he just as crazy?"

"I don't know, but please stop him from whatever he is doing."

Standing straight, I twist the handle and push it open. The screams are coming from the second door. Pushing it open, a young guy, not much older than me, sits in a chair, his arms and legs strapped in, and his mouth gagged. He looks up at me with his big brown eyes.

The scream fills the room, and I spin, smiling when I see the small speaker.

"Smart, really. I know they don't like hurting innocent people, but I wonder what your sister did. Would you tell me if I ungagged you?"

A throat clears, and I pivot to see a man with so many muscles my eyes don't know where to look first. Holy crap, Kill's brother is hot for an old guy.

"I wouldn't do that if I were you."

I smile at the man. "But I'm not you, and I hate they won't tell me shit because they think that I'm a kid."

The man leans against the wall, his arms crossed over his chest. "You do look like a child to me, but something in your eyes says the things you have been through have made you a lot more mature than your age suggests."

"Thank you. Will you tell me where everyone is and why Cat is hanging up like a slab of meat?"

"Your sister is missing, and Cat is behind it, and she even helped my sister murder my wife and children."

I gasp. "Jordyn is missing, and your sister killed your family?"

He nods. "Yup, Enzo has found your sister, or knows where she is. That is where they have gone, and my sister won't make it through the night. I'm enjoying this too much but looking at her makes me want to just end her. But she has her own children. Does that make me as bad as her?"

I shrug. "It seems like she deserves it, and kids bounce back. I didn't need my mom, just one person who loved me. I always had Jordyn. Do they have a father, maybe he will take them in?"

He shrugs. "I haven't seen Fiona or Kill since we were kids. I don't know all that much about them, but I kept some tabs on their location so they didn't come to kill me in my sleep."

"So why are they keeping Cat alive if she took my sister?"

He shrugs again. "Okay, well, I'm going back upstairs to wait for my sister to come home. Happy Murdering Your Sister Day." I give him two thumbs up.

"Thank you."

He pushes off the wall and leaves the room, but then he

puts his head back in. "The kid stays strapped to the chair until they are done with the girl, then, he will go home."

I nod and face the boy again. "Don't be scared, they won't hurt you. I'm sorry your sister has lost it."

He looks so sad, and his sister is not a good person. Enzo will be in his head about killing a family friend, and Sarge won't touch her. I know Kill will do what needs to be done.

Leaving the room, I go back to where Cat is. "What are they doing to my brother?"

"Lots of electricity, and the burns, so bad. It would just be easier to talk."

She scoffs. "As if I would. I thought working with his mother would make him see how good I would be in this life. Selling children, not my first choice."

The hairs on the back of my neck stand on end; the knife sitting on the metal counter gleams under the lights. Lev said I needed to be sure I could live with myself before taking someone's life, that your first kill is the worst. Regret eats away at you, that small part of you wondering if you made the right choice. Maybe if I kill Cat, I can show him that I am strong enough to go after the men who hurt me, that I'm not a kid.

Tunnel vision leads me to the knife, Kill's favorite throwing blade; it's ended up in the wall by the door so many times the wood is splinted with divots. When I turn, Cat's eyes widen before she composes herself.

"Put the knife down, you're a child."

Anger floods me, a fucking child. "I'm not a child," I snap. "Stop saying that, you're one of the reasons I was taken, you admitted it. Do you know what they did to me? Maybe I should explain it to you."

Stepping closer to her, I run the knife down her stomach. The blade slices the thin material of her tight red dress easily.

"They touched me," I whisper, "Places no one has. They wanted to train me. Lev tried to convince them to leave me a virgin and that I would fetch a higher price, but no, Bear wanted me broken in. He had a buyer in mind, one who likes obedience because he wants girls' fear. Do you know what it's like to be so scared you just wished you would die?"

Pushing the blade harder, it breaks her skin. "I'm sorry, I didn't think about what they were doing to you."

Manic laughter bellows out of me. She didn't think. Of course, she didn't. She just wanted Enzo so badly that she would do anything to get him, and I can understand that, but she did it at my expense, and my sister is the best person I know. She sacrificed her whole life for me. It's why I went to see my mom, to tell her how royally that she fucked up, and to make her understand what Jordyn went through. The older I got; I knew what those men were doing to her. I did what she said, hid under my bed until the footsteps went back down the hall, and she would crawl into bed with me and hold me. She is my savior, and I will do this for her.

I rear back my hand and plunge the knife into her stomach. "That's for my sister."

Back and forth, over and over again. There's something so cathartic about seeing the blood drip to the floor and pool beneath her feet.

"And when you take your last breath, that is for me."

Movement snaps me out of my head, and I look down at my hand and drop the knife. My eyes snap up to see Jordyn and Harper standing at the door. Jordyn stumbles into the room and pulls my shaky body into her arms.

"Shh, it will be okay."

"I'm sorry," I cry. "She...she told me she was one of the ones who wanted to sell me, and Kill's brother told me you were missing because of her, and Lev's words were in my head. He said the first is the worst, but I don't feel bad that she is dead. I don't. That dickhead husband can send me away."

"Look at me," Jordyn says. "He won't send you away, I promise. How about you come with Harper and me, and we get you cleaned up?"

I nod. I can do that. Looking over at Cat one last time, her head hangs and she looks so peaceful, as if she is sleeping. I don't understand what Lev is talking about at all. The men on my list better count the days they have left on this earth. I will get stronger, and they won't see me coming until they are begging for mercy.

CHAPTER TWENTY-THREE

ENZO

The Irish bastards pull up to the curb in front of the abandoned house in Huntersville. I wasn't exactly happy that Kill brought them home. We have never been enemies; they stay in their territory, and I stay in mine. It doesn't mean that I want to work alongside them. Kill and I need to sit down and have a long chat. I don't care if he is somehow related to them, he needs to choose, and it's time he takes the oath. We have too much on the line now. Jordyn and Mars need to come first.

Thinking about Jordyn, my heart beats erratically in my chest, and I try to even out my breathing. What if she isn't okay, or they hurt her?

"Breathe," Sarge says, putting his hand on my arm as he pulls up behind Ronan's SUV. Kill barely waits for the car to stop before he jumps out, his gun firmly in his hand. He isn't one who likes to use bullets in a fight, but he won't take any risks where it involves our girl.

Ronan and his posse follow Kill's lead. Sarge nods at me,

and we both exit the car. Kill points to the sides of the house, and the Irish split up. They're going around the back, and we will take the front.

Kill kicks in the front door, and it crumbles beneath the force. He fires his gun, and a man slumps to the floor, then Sarge moves in and checks the man's pulse.

Ronan quickly joins us. The house isn't big, and the sweep takes them two seconds. "Boss," one of the others says. "You need to come see this."

We follow Ronan down a set of stairs, where Darragh is squatting beside a dead man. "Looks like his throat was slit with something."

"What about that one?" Sarge asks, pointing to the second man.

Cian uses his boot and kicks the man from his side, and his body falls flat on his back. It is then we can see the mark on his face. Someone hit him really hard. I guess one hit really can kill.

My phone starts to vibrate; it's the house line. "Ugh, Boss, we have a situation."

I put the call on speaker; as much as I don't want the Irish bastards to know my business, we are kind of in this one together.

"What situation, Milo?"

He exhales. "Cat is dead, Pixie went all psycho on her, and Jordyn and Harper are back. Jordyn is refusing to go get checked, Harper is yelling, and I think she has broken ribs. Pike is trying to diffuse the situation. We need you here."

"On my way," I say, ending the call.

Kill laughs. "Of course, they saved themselves. Our girl is no damsel in distress."

Sarge nudges him with his arm. "It would be nice to be the knight just once, though."

Cian smiles. "Let's go get our women. No disrespect, Italian, but we are taking her."

I nod and fucking smile at him. "None taken, Irish, just don't piss her off. I would hate to have to kill you."

Ronan laughs as we walk up the stairs. "I'm sure you would lose so much sleep over it."

Kill breaks off from the pack, but who the fuck knows what he is doing. We all wait out by the cars, and when we see smoke, that's when we realize what he is doing.

He comes out the front door with a small pep in his step, and when he reaches the curb, he turns around and looks at the house like he is waiting for something. But before I can ask, the entire house blows up.

With a smile on his lips, he slips into the backseat. Both Sarge and I follow his lead. The drive back to the house is quiet. I can only guess they feel what I do, relief that Jordyn is okay but a small sense of annoyance that we were not the ones to save the day. I know it sounds messed up, but I got her into this mess, and I wanted to be the one to fix it.

"Before we get home, what are we going to do with Pixie?" Kill asks, leaning forward.

I grind my teeth together. "What can we do? We need to leave this one up to Jordyn," Sarge says.

"Can we ship her off to boarding school or something? Who fucking knew teenage girls were this hard to deal with?" I ask; it's a legitimate option right now.

Kill snorts. "At least the issue of who gets to kill Cat is dealt with. You know that I would have done it, but at least you don't have to really lie to her father. Even though I still vote that you sit him down and put his entire family on a very thin leash."

I sigh. "I will put Angelo in charge of this one. He has been helping Dad and my uncles a lot. I think he wants to prove himself."

I look at Sarge, and he shrugs. "Your call."

Before long, we are pulling up into the driveway. Killian jumps from the car when Cian walks out of our front door with Harper over his shoulder, and she is kicking and screaming.

"Put me down, you son of a bitch, my best friend needs me."

Sarge pushes past us all when Jordyn stands in the doorway. She launches herself at him, and he wraps his arms around her. Both Kill and I nod, understanding Sarge needs this moment right now.

Cian lets Harper slide down his body but pulls her in tight. "Angel, right now, we need you. First, you vanish on us, then we find out you were assaulted. Someone dared to touch what belongs to me. Then you were kidnapped. Don't fucking push me right now. I'm on the edge of exploding. Killian has Ronan's number. He can call you with an update."

Darragh walks out of the house with two girls plastered to his chest. That makes Killian step forward.

"Where the fuck are you taking my nieces?"

Darragh just ignores Kill and keeps walking. Ronan quickly moves to Kill's side and places a hand on his shoulder that Kill shrugs off. "He just found out the girls are his daughters. He needs some time. Ask your brother to fill you in."

"Who was watching those children while we were gone?" I ask. I had completely forgotten they were even here.

"Pike," Kill replies. I shake my head. Of course, he would leave children in the hands of a man who could kill them. I will have to remind myself to make sure he is never in charge of finding a sitter.

Ronan comes to stand in front of me and holds out his hand. I look down at it before taking his hand in mine. "If you need anything."

"I won't, but thank you."

Turning back to see where Jordyn is, she is looking up at Kill, a smile so wide on her face, but she hesitates until he pulls her into his chest, and she wraps her arms around his waist. When she pulls back, he steps aside, and her eyes meet mine, and everything else around me ceases to exist. I haven't wanted to allow myself to really fall in deep with anyone over the years. Love is a weakness, one that could kill you. But as I move my feet closer to her, I don't care if she is the beginning of the end, I couldn't think of another person I would rather die for. Right here, right now, I know that walking into that brothel was the best choice I have ever made in my life.

"Hi," she whispers when we are standing so close that I can feel her stomach against mine.

"Hi back."

"I think we need to go to the hospital, but I need a favor first."

She looks down at her stomach, but I take her chin and make her look up at me. "Anything for you."

"Please don't bring up Cat around Pixie. I want to be the

one, but Mars needs me right now. Can you call your father to come watch her? She really likes him."

"Ten steps ahead of you," Sarge says. "I messaged him before we left Huntersville, he should be here any minute."

Milo comes bursting out of the front door with a duffle bag in his hand and a small suitcase. He trips over his own feet and flies headfirst down the stairs, springs up to his feet, and dusts himself off. "Your bags. Pixie wanted me to bring them down and to say good luck. Go, she will be fine. I will make sure of it."

Jordyn steps forward, pulls Milo into her, and gives him a hug. Kill grumbles about murdering him, and she steps back.

"Speaking of, all the people need to be moved before they start to smell," I say, and his face lights up. "And call Angelo and tell him to return Cat's brother to his family."

"On it...wait. On second thought, that big guy down there isn't going to murder me, will he?"

Kill chuckles. It's quite concerning how he makes chills run up your spine when he does it. "Only one way to find out."

Jordyn whacks him in the chest. "You will be fine, and thank you for keeping an eye on Pix. Mario will be here soon to take over."

Sarge pushes past us and takes the bags. "Let's fucking go. Mars is too early to come, and we need to get him checked out."

I guess we are off to the hospital to get my son and my wife checked over. Immediately, panic starts to set in. I don't know anything about being a father, or how to even look after a newborn. I'm the head of the D'Arco family, I know how to end a man's life in every way that's possible, but how the hell do I change a diaper? Will they come with an instruction manual, what happens when they cry? So many things I should have researched before today, but stupidly thought that I would have more time.

Lost in thought, I stare out the window as Sarge drives us to the hospital, where Lucia is going to meet us. How the fuck do I tell her that her sister is dead? I have known these women since I was a little boy. She never really liked her sister, but I can't imagine she would have wanted her dead.

Sarge interlocks his hand with mine, and I feel all the tension leave my body. I don't know how he does it, but he just knows when I need him; he always has.

"I can't wait to watch you fuck," Jordyn says from the back seat. Sarge chokes on his own spit and looks at her through the rear vision mirror, and I turn my body so I can look back at her.

"I'm not even into the whole man-on-man, but I think I'm with you. All that tension has been building."

Sarge bellows out a laugh, and I reply, "You know I like an audience. My door is always open."

The rest of the drive is lighthearted until we find a parking spot, and Sarge opens Jordyn's door and tries to pull her into his arms.

"I can walk, you know," she snaps at him and tries to swat him away, but his sheer determination and size makes him a force to be reckoned with. He scoops her up into his arms, and Kill and I grab the bags.

"You're going to drop me; my fat ass weighs a ton."

Sarge just laughs it off but Kill falls in step with them. "Poppet, put yourself down one more time and I will bend you over and eat your fucking ass in front of everyone. Anyone game enough to watch dies."

I shake my head at him because I know that he will do just that if she pushes him. I wish she could see herself through our eyes. She is perfect, even if she has a big stomach and swollen ankles. I have never seen anything so beautiful in my entire life.

CHAPTER TWENTY-FOUR

JORDYN

I stick to my original statement of who the fuck would do this more than once. After I was admitted and given steroid shots for Mars's lungs, they hooked me up to give me an IV so I didn't get an infection since they said it was definitely my water that broke.

The pain is unlike anything I have ever felt before. "Killian! Take me back to the torture chamber, this shit fucking sucks."

Killian pushes up off the chair that he is sitting in and switches out with Sarge, who moves to the foot of the bed and starts to massage my feet.

"Poppet, you know I would in a heartbeat, but this little guy needs to come out one way or another."

"Another," I demand. "Just cut him out, please. And where is the man with the drugs? They said he would be here."

"Lucia said the anaesthesiologist will be here soon."

Reaching up, I twist Enzo's shirt between my fingers and

drag him down to my level. "Soon is not good enough... agh fuck, another one."

I close my eyes and try to breathe through the pain. When I open my eyes, my midwife, Lucy, flits into the room. I want to throat-punch her and her peppy attitude.

"How are we doing?" she asks.

"Take a wild stab in the dark. How do you think I'm doing? I need drugs and lots of them."

She doesn't get to answer before the machine attached to my stomach starts to go crazy. She walks over to the machine, and her brows furrow.

"I will be back in a minute," she says as she hastily leaves the room. I watch her leave and turn back to Enzo.

"Where is she going? What does the machine say?"

Sarge walks over to the machine and stares at the paper for a minute. "If I had to guess, it looks like Mars's heart rate is dropping."

My heart sinks into my stomach. "Enzo, so help me God, if you don't go and find out what is going on right now!"

Enzo nods, and before he leaves the room, Lucy is back with an older man, probably not a great deal older than Killian, but he shows his age with his salt-and-pepper hair.

"Mrs. D'Arco, it seems that the baby is a little unhappy, and we would like to..."

"Just cut him out. If you don't, I will make him do it."

Pointing to Kill makes the doctor's eyes go as wide as saucers, and Killian fucking smiles at me.

"Then let's prep you for a c-section."

Thank God, I can't bear the thought of something happening to him. I need to know that he is safe and in my arms.

It doesn't take long before my men are in gowns, and I am ready to be wheeled into the operating room. Nerves eat away at me the longer it takes. The doctor had to run through all the risks, and I am woman enough to know that they scare me. Sarge holds my hand, and I'm grateful he has a way of calming me down.

"Just remember," the doctor says. "Stay out of the way, or we will ask you to leave. I'm bending rules for you."

"Don't act as if you have a choice right now. Do your fucking job, and well."

"Enzo," I snap, "Now is not the time to threaten the doctor."

Enzo nods. "Sorry, Doc, nerves."

I shake my head. He didn't even mean it. Finally, I'm wheeled in, and everything feels so sterile. I'm extra glad when they put up a divider so I can't see what they are doing. Sarge stands beside me and holds my hand, while Killian says that he wants to see the action, and Enzo stands near the divider so that he can watch but also be close to me.

"Do you think I can make the first incision?" Killian asks the doctor. One of the nurses laughs, but she shouldn't, he is dead serious.

"I don't think that is a good idea, but you can watch."

Time goes so slowly; it feels like there is never going to be a baby. My body starts to shake. Sarge squeezes my hand.

"You're doing so well."

Am I? All I'm doing is laying here, unable to move, useless. Minute after minute passes until the doctor holds the baby up, I see him for a split second before he is taken away.

Enzo looks down at me with tears in his eyes. "Did you see all of his hair?"

Cries fill the room, and strangely, I feel like I can finally breathe. A nurse brings him to me, wrapped in a blanket, and places him on my chest.

The moment he blinks his little eyes open and looks at me, I understand what unconditional love feels like, and tears slide down my face. Did my mother feel this sense of joy with me and my sister? Because if she did, there is no way that she would have treated us the way she did. I'm going to protect this baby with my life and do anything I have to just to keep him safe.

"He is perfect," I whisper. "Welcome to the world, Mars Andrew Masters D'Arco."

The whole world vanishes while I stare at the most beautiful thing in the world. Hours could have passed, and I wouldn't have noticed, and I didn't until the nurse asked if she could take Mars while I was taken back to my room. Hesitantly, she takes him from my arms when I nod my head. Sarge hasn't moved from my side, and Enzo has been on the phone with his father and my sister, who I even heard congratulate him but still managed to call him a dickhead. Killian has been quiet; I wish I could read his mind.

They took Mars to the nursery to make sure he was okay. Being born early, there could have been complications, but when the nurse brought him back in and said he was perfect, I cried like a baby just having him back. She did say she would have to come back and check, but for now, he is allowed to stay in my room.

Killian leans against the far wall, Enzo cradles Mars in his arms, and Sarge is squatted down in front of him, both totally smitten. I hold my hand out to Killian, and he pushes off the wall and comes to my side.

"What's wrong? You're quiet."

He shrugs. "Just thinking. I never imagined that I would want to protect someone as much as I do you. But when they pulled him from you, which was the best thing I have seen in my entire life, you all cut open like that, I held my breath until he cried and, at that moment, I knew that if I had to choose between you and him, I would definitely throw you in front of the danger to save him."

He smirks at me, and I slap his arm. "Can we throw Enzo first before me? I'm more useful."

He takes my hand in his and lifts it to his mouth, pressing a kiss to my skin. "I love you, Poppet, and I never thought I would have a real family again. You complete that. I'm ready."

He coughs to cover up the fact that he is choked up. "You're ready?" I ask, and he nods.

"To take the oath, to belong to one place."

I look from Killian to Enzo, who is now watching us, and he hands Mars to Sarge, who holds my son like he is the most precious thing in the world. Enzo stands and moves closer to us. He stops close to Killian, who freezes, and Enzo pulls him into a man hug. Killian just stands there awkwardly.

"This doesn't mean I will fuck you," Enzo says lightheartedly, and Killian pushes him away and laughs.

"In your dreams. I reserve all of this for my woman."

"Are you trying to replace me already?" Sarge asks. "If you need me to get a little freaky like Kill, I will bring a knife to bed."

We all laugh at the light banter between us. A knock on the door has the laughter pause, and my sister pops her head into the room, followed by Harper and Ronan. Enzo straightens up; he won't let his guard down around a rival family, even if they are on friendly-ish terms.

My sister runs straight over to Sarge and Mars, while Ronan shakes Enzo's hand. Harper comes to my side.

"Congratulations. You did it," she says, smiling down at me.

"I did," I say, lowering my voice. "Is everything okay with..." I angle my head toward Ronan, who looks so uncomfortable standing so close to Enzo.

Harper nods. "Yeah, I will be fine. It's complicated, but right now, you don't need to worry about me. You just had a freaking baby cut out of you."

Placing my hand on hers, I murmur, "I will always worry about you. You're my person."

Harper tears up and leans down to hug me. Never in my wildest dreams did I think that I would be the first to have a baby. Harper has always been the one to believe in the fairy-tale life, not that she believed she would ever find it, but she loves the concept of it. Maybe she will find that in the most unlikely of places, just like I have.

CHAPTER TWENTY-FIVE

SARGE

Pacing the foyer was not the plan, but I can't help it because Jordyn and Mars come home today. They had to stay in the hospital longer. Mars came out strong, but he was still early and had some feeding issues, and he turned yellow, which was jaundice. I never knew that was a thing with babies. I have spent the time they've been away making sure the nursery was set up and our new room since the renovations finished.

Killian has been keeping himself busy in the basement to avoid me. He also seems a little depressed since Pike left. He would never admit it, but I think they bonded for the first time ever.

Cat's funeral was last week, and Enzo made a stand and refused to attend. Mario went since he and the Mancini family were close and to show respect to an old friend. That is now where the relationship between the families ends. Enzo has made that very clear. No one threatens his family and gets away with it. No one knows it was Pixie who killed her, and no one ever will. If they decide to retaliate, we will never put a child in the firing line.

"If you don't stop pacing, you will wear a hole in the floor," Pixie says, coming down the stairs. How the hell does this kid go through hell and back and still be so peppy?

"They should have been back by now, what if something went wrong?"

She closes the space between us and wraps her arms around my middle. "They would have called you. Calm down."

I wrap my arms around her and place a kiss on her head. "Thank you. Is everything good with you?"

"Yes, I'm going on a date with Finn. Enzo allowed it since Harper will be driving us."

"Make sure he is a gentleman; I don't need Kill murdering a teenager, and we both know he will."

Pixie chuckles against my chest. "You don't have anything to worry about. If he isn't a gentleman, I can use those moves you have been teaching me on him."

She pulls back from our hug and does some made-up karate moves, which makes me laugh. Tires on the driveway make me abandon the conversation and race for the door, ready to welcome them home. My heart sinks when it's the wrong SUV pulling up.

A redheaded kid with freckles and a smile as big as his face jumps out of the car with a bunch of flowers and walks toward the door. Harper and Sullivan also get out, and Harp gives me a wave.

Pixie casually walks out of the door. "You look absolutely

breathtaking," the kid says, and Pixie giggles as he hands her the flowers.

"Thank you." She hands the flowers to me. "Sarge, put these in water for me."

The kid offers her his arm and turns away. "Have her back at a decent hour. And no under-the-clothes stuff or Kill will use your hands as paperweights."

Pixie turns back and flips me off. I watch as she slips into the car, and they drive away. My excitement peaks when my SUV pulls up to the gates and is buzzed in. Enzo has upped his security now that he's a dad. The fence is electric and looks like a prison. All the entries are now hand scanners. Motion sensors have been added inside the house and can only be deactivated by knowing where the panels are. He is taking no chances with Mars coming home. Every room in the house now has scanners as well. So, in the case that someone gets through the gates and into the main doors, the bedrooms are all safe and have emergency buttons that bring in not only the security on duty but a whole backup team.

Enzo has the whole family now working to be stronger than ever and bringing in some new soldiers. Angelo has stepped up and is helping Enzo a lot while he has been at the hospital with Jordyn and Mars.

Enzo pulls the car right up to the front of the house, and I race around to the back passenger seat, knowing Jordyn would want to sit right next to our baby. Opening the door, I offer her my hand and help her out of the car slowly.

"I'm fine," she says, but I don't care if she wants to act tough. She has three men at her beck and call, she doesn't ever need to walk again if she doesn't want to. One of us would happily help her.

"Where is everyone?" Enzo asks as he unclips Mars's baby car seat.

I laugh. "Your dad told everyone that you get home tomorrow. Your aunts are like blow flies and won't stop. He wanted you to be able to relax. He has also made sure that everyone has had their shots, purchased a million bottles of hand sanitizer, and told anyone who smokes not to bother coming if they smell. He is taking his grandparent duties to the extreme. Did you know he has social media? He posted about it. He is crazy."

Enzo laughs as he overtakes us. Jordyn grasps my hand as we slowly reach the stairs. Kill runs outside and goes to her other side.

"I feel like an invalid with you both fussing over me."

"Just accept our help, we don't know what else to do. I can carry you if you like."

The sound of her laughter lights up my insides and gives me the warm and fuzzies. It's been a hell of a long time since I allowed myself to enjoy life.

Kaser meets us in the foyer; he is back at work but on light duties, and he is in charge of the online security system.

"Boss, there is a visitor at the gate."

Enzo puts Mars's seat on the ground and starts to unclip him. "Who?"

"Mrs. D'Arco's mother."

Enzo looks at Jordyn, who freezes. "Did you want her to meet Mars? Just remember, she can't hurt you anymore or Pixie."

Jordyn nods. "Let her in. Bring her to the sitting room. I need to feed Mars."

Kaser nods and radios down to the gate as he walks

through the front doors. I help Jordyn into the sitting room, and she takes a seat on the couch.

Enzo whips out the baby bag and change mat like an old pro and starts to change Mars's diaper.

Holy cow, how does one small baby make that much poop? It's beyond me. Once Enzo has him all cleaned up, he hands him to Jordyn.

"Can you run upstairs and get the breast-feeding pillow?" she asks Kill. He nods and goes upstairs while Jordyn coos and smiles at Mars. I join her, taking a seat to her left.

Kill is back in a flash with the pillow. "Can you take him for a second?" she asks me, and I hold my arms out and take him. He is so small, and I could smell him all day long. I have set up a newborn photoshoot next week. I couldn't help myself. Enzo laughed at me when I had a lady come into the hospital to do hand and foot castings for memories. I don't want to forget anything.

One day, I would love to have a child of my own, but right now, I am content. I have an amazing girlfriend and a son, even if he isn't biologically mine. I won't treat him any differently, and I never imagined I would say I also had a boyfriend, not that we have put labels on it. Enzo likes to growl *mine* a lot like a caveman.

Cal walks into the sitting room, along with Kaser and Sophie, Jordyn's mother. Cal takes one look toward Jordyn and spins around.

"Nope, I'm out and will go watch the grass grow for a bit. I don't need to die today. Once in Kill's basement was enough for me."

"I will join you," Kill says. He isn't a fan of people

watching Jordyn breastfeed. His inner beast wants to skin them alive.

Kaser follows them out as well. Sophie slowly moves into the room. Jordyn hasn't spoken to her mother in a long time. I want to excuse myself, but she digs her nails into my leg. If she wants me here, then I will stay.

"I need to go and make some calls. Will you be good here?" Enzo asks Jordyn, and she nods.

"I'm so nervous," Sophie says, taking a seat opposite us. "I played this moment over and over again in my head until Pixie came to see me, and she made me realize my apology is just words. And now I don't know how to act."

Jordyn bites her lip and looks down at Mars, and then back to her mom. "How about we start fresh? We can't change the past, and I hate dwelling on it. But it will be a while until we are good or if I even trust you. That is earned."

Sophie nods. "Thank you. I don't deserve a second chance after what I put you through, but I'm so grateful to Killian. He could have just killed me."

Jordyn raises a brow at her mother. Kill never straight out told her about sending her mother away. I'm sure it's been mentioned, but always when something else has been going on.

"He spared me. I think it was when he realized I was your mom, he sent me to live with Cal. The first week was tough, and Cal had to lock me ironically in his basement to get through withdrawals. God knows, I probably would have run otherwise. I'm good now, though, and I love living out there on the land, away from everything. It's soothing."

"It's not some weird cult, is it?" Jordyn asks, and Sophie laughs.

"Oh no, it's just a group of people like me that Cal has helped. We grow our own food, and it's really just like an extended camping trip. We don't worship Cal or anything like that."

Mars finishes feeding, and Jordyn brings him up to her shoulder and lightly pats his back until he burps. He lets one rip straight away.

"Would you like to hold him?" Jordyn asks her mom, and she nods. I jump up and take him, and Sophie has her arm ready to support his head. She smiles down at him, and tears slide down her face.

"Do you like being a mom?"

Jordyn nods. "I do. I never wanted children, and I still don't understand why people do it more than once. Maybe a little now that he's here. I'm just lucky I have three men to help me out."

"Cal did tell me about that, and I'm happy for you. You deserve all the happiness in the world. There is no way I can ever repay you for raising Pixie or even yourself. I have no doubt that you will be the best mom in the world. Mars is a very lucky boy."

I ease my way out of the room as the women talk. This is good for Jordyn and her healing from the past of her trauma. Nothing Sophie can ever do or say will change the past, but the future is wide open, and I know Jordyn wants Mars to have the life she didn't, full of love and family and lucky for her, there is nothing that Enzo, Kill, or I want more than to be a family with her. To give Mars what we didn't have.

Enzo was lucky and has all the family any of us could need, and they all accept us. All I need to do now is convince them that we need a whole house full of children. I can't see that being an easy task, but you just never know what the future holds.

CHAPTER TWENTY-SIX

KILLIAN

Watching the screen, I track Pike's movements. When he left, he didn't tell me. He left me a note that said he had killed Fiona and was taking her body to give her a burial. He didn't ask me to take the device out of his neck, and it wasn't even an explosive. Just a tracking device, one I could probably have blown up if I needed to, but I'm not sure it would exactly blow his entire head off, even if that would be fucking amazing. I should pay someone to create something like that for me.

Knowing where to find my sister's body is a relief. Jordyn has changed me; I know I should feel something more about my sister's death, but I don't. I don't feel sad or happy, it just is what it is.

I could have ended Pike's life; I should have ended his life. Living without his wife and children would be hell on earth. I wouldn't have understood that before Jordyn, but now, if anyone took her or Mars from me, I would have instantly done something insane that would end me. My entire day starts and ends with Jordyn. I never imagined that I could feel the things I do for a woman. I spent my entire life despising women for the act of one. Pretty fucking messed up if you ask me.

Sarge walks into the basement and flops himself down onto the chair by the desk. He has decided that every time Mars wakes up, he will get up as well, even though Enzo and Jordyn suggested that we all take turns since there are three of us. But the sappy bastard doesn't want to miss anything.

"Do you know how much waiting six weeks sucks?" he asks. Ah yes, when the doctor realized that all three of us were with Jordyn, he tried to make it very clear we needed to abstain from sex to give her body a chance to recover.

"Don't even pretend that you and Enzo are not fucking in the shower."

He throws his head back and laughs. "If you're jealous, I'm sure Enzo would let you join in."

"Fuck you," I say, launching my carving knife toward him. It flies above his head and wedges into the wooden shelf above him. "I'm a patient man. I would rather wait until I can bury myself in our woman."

This all gives me an idea. The doctor said we couldn't fuck her, but he never said anything about orgasms.

"I should head upstairs; Mars is getting ready for bed." He pushes up off the seat.

"I will be up in a sec. We have a rat coming in. Apparently, he has had loose lips about our business dealings."

Sarge nods and heads back upstairs. Anyone brought here now has to come through the basement door. No one shady is allowed to step foot through the front door. The buzzer lights up the room now since sometimes I listen to music so loud I can't hear the knock at the door. I move across the room and open the door. One of the soldiers pushes a weedy-looking kid through the door with a sack over his head.

"I think he pissed his pants on the way over," he says. I nod, and when he realizes that I have nothing more to say, he steps back, and I shut the door, ripping the sack off the guy's head.

Just in time, I hear the sound of the main basement door opening, and Milo appears. "You wanted me?"

I did. I sent him a text to meet me here, and he is right on time. "Yep, this is your first shot at extracting information. Shouldn't be a hard job. I do not want to be distracted tonight, so do what needs to be done. Any tools you get bloody, you wash."

A smile takes over his face. I don't know if I have seen anyone that genuinely happy about this job, but Milo is a different breed of idiot.

I push the man toward Milo. "Yes, boss, I won't let you down."

I shrug. "No skin off my nose if you do, I will just come back and kill him."

Milo still hasn't wiped the smile off his face as he pulls the chains down from the ceiling and gets to work. I watch until the man is secure, and I leave him to it. I have a woman to service and two men who can sit back and watch since they have each other to fondle.

Heading upstairs, I find Mario in the living room with Pixie and Mars. Mario glances over at me. "Saying goodnight to the grandchildren before I head out."

I shake my head. The man is here every morning and every night; he spends as much time as he can with the kids.

"Actually, can I ask you for a favor, would you watch Mars for a little bit longer?"

Mario smiles back at me, and Pixie looks between us. "Gross, seriously, Kill."

I just shrug. "I would love to. Any excuse to be with the handsome little man. And if you ask me, he looks just like me."

"I can see it," Pixie says. "Mars has that old man look about him."

Mario fake gasps. "Old man? I might need to reconsider that horse I was thinking of buying you for your birthday."

"Did I say old? I meant mature."

That makes me laugh. "I will leave you and your maturity down here. There are diapers and spare clothes under the table in the drawers, and if he gets hungry, there is expressed milk in the refrigerator. Sarge likes to do a feed at night."

Mario waves me off, and I take the stairs two at a time and find Jordyn in the shower. I take a deep breath as I kick my boots off. Being completely naked leaves me vulnerable, and it's still something I am working on. With each item of clothing I pull off, I remind myself that it's Jordyn. My scars don't make her pity me. To her, they are the battle wounds that lead us to each other. If one small part of our past was different, we wouldn't have met, and to me, every ounce of pain I endured to get to her was worth it, and I would go through it all again.

Opening the glass shower door, steam piles out and she looks over, and her eyes widen when she realizes that it's me.

"Killian, what a nice surprise. I was just about to get out. Mario is watching Mars while I shower."

I step all the way in and close the door. "Mars is fine," I say before dropping to my knees in front of her, grabbing her leg before she can protest, and lifting it over my shoulder.

"Oh fuck," she gasps as I lean in and suck one of her pussy lips into my mouth. She bucks her hips forward and tangles her fingers in my hair.

Savage is the word that comes to mind right now. I savagely eat her perfect cunt. I didn't think anyone could have a perfect pussy, but she does. Everything is neatly tucked inside, and the gem from her clit bar sits just at the top, and I like to think of it as my own personal jewelry box. All the most precious pieces inside.

"Yes, Kill, fuck me with your tongue. Please, don't stop."

I doubt Jordyn feels the change in the air, but I feel it, the shift in temperature. Someone has just walked into the ensuite. Lifting two fingers, I slowly insert them inside her as I suck her clit into my mouth.

The shower door opens, and Sarge steps in. "Cheeky bastard, thought we were waiting six weeks?"

"Oh, we are," I say, pulling my head back. "It just occurred to me that he said nothing about orgasms."

"Why is my father setting up camp with our child in the living room? The guy is crazy. He is setting up a fucking fort, I mean, Mars is a few weeks old. Oh, never mind, now I know."

I laugh against Jordyn's pussy. The shower is big, but it is certainly not four people big.

"Let's move this into the bedroom, but you fuckers are watching," I say, moving myself out from under Jordyn's leg.

She doesn't waste any time as she steps out of the shower and Enzo holds up a towel for her, wraps it around her body, and they leave the ensuite. Both Sarge and I do the same. Sarge wraps a towel around his waist, and I pat myself dry.

Stepping out of the ensuite, I come to a complete stop. Jordyn is lying on the bed naked, her legs spread. Both Enzo and Sarge are as enamored as I am. We all stand side by side. She pushes up on her elbows and smirks, pulling out a purple vibrator and waves it in the air.

I step forward; I'm in charge of this one. "On your hands and knees, Jordyn."

She smirks and gets on her hands and knees as I get some pillows and help put them under her stomach. I don't want to risk hurting her.

"Here is what is going to happen, you two lover boys better put on a good show for our girl, keep her distracted. I'm going to eat her ass and let the vibrator work her up. I want her so wet she drowns me."

CHAPTER TWENTY-SEVEN

JORDYN

I have been patient, waiting for them to come to me. The doctor said six weeks to allow my body a chance to heal, but I feel fine. I even had a chance to order a vibrator online. Harper helped me pick the right one. The plan was to self-service and hope they walked in, but Killian beat me to it.

He tucks some pillows under my stomach, which helps hold my stomach and stop it wobbling, and I'm grateful for it. I feel him behind me and hear him switch the vibrator on. Harper said to keep it simple since she doubted they would hold back once they figured it out.

He runs the vibrator down my spine slowly while I keep my eyes locked on Enzo and Sarge, waiting to see what they will do. Enzo loosens his tie and drops to his knees, slowly pulling the towel from around Sarge's waist until it falls to the floor. I miss the feel of his cock, and anticipation swirls in my gut as Enzo's tongue runs up Sarge's shaft.

"Fuck," I whisper, and my core clenches. Killian must be listening to my breathing, the more rapid it becomes from watching Enzo suck cock deep into his mouth, the closer he brings the vibrator to where it needs to be.

He brings the vibrator down my ass crack until it's sitting over my hole. My pussy contracts trying the best she can to suck it inside and give some relief, but he swirls it around, lightly teasing me, bringing me pleasure I didn't think was possible without penetration.

When Enzo stands, I watch to see what he is going to do. He pushes against Sarge's pecs, and he steps backward until he reaches the bed.

"Lean over the bed and spread your legs."

Sarge does as Enzo asks, first leaning in and pressing a kiss to my lips. It's quick and sweet. His eyes always give away so much more than his words. He is making sure I'm okay with this. We have spoken about Enzo and Sarge's relationship in detail, and they don't want it to distract from their relationship with me. I'm so fucking horny right now, knowing I get to watch this, seeing them come together.

I have waited, having asked them to explore together in private, to give themselves time, and now they are clearly ready to share.

Enzo kicks Sarge's legs further apart and brings his hand down hard against his ass while Killian tongues my ass. It's such an unusual feeling, but I want it, I want to take two of them at once one day.

Enzo flips the cap open on a tube of lube and squirts it down Sarge's ass crack and throws the tube close to Killian and smiles.

I suck my ass cheeks together. No way am I ready for Killian's monster in there; he almost splits my pussy in half when we fuck.

"Relax, Poppet, I will start with a finger."

Nodding, I push my ass back. A finger I can do. He squirts lube on my crack and uses his fingers to smear it everywhere, teasing me.

Enzo rips a foil packet open, and I watch as he slides it down his length and steps back behind Sarge. So many sensations overwhelm me at once; Sarge's face as Enzo pushes in is almost pure bliss, and the feeling of Killian pushing a finger inside me. Once he is in, he stops, giving me a chance to adapt.

"Put the vibrator between the pillows and your clit."

He hands me the vibrator, and it's already set on the lowest speed. I reach underneath myself and wedge the thing like he asks; the tip touching my clit. If I move, it will fall, so I keep still as Killian's finger starts to move in and out of me, and just as Enzo starts to move, Sarge takes my hands in his.

"You're so beautiful," he whispers.

An orgasm quickly starts to build with the constant vibrations sending shock waves to my clit. It's swollen, and I know I have the lady equivalent of blue balls.

When a second finger is added to my ass, I feel the slight burn before it becomes pleasurable.

"Fuck, your ass is tight," Enzo grunts, bringing his hand down hard on Sarge's ass, causing me to clench around Killian's fingers.

"Watching you two is so fucking hot. Come for me, Sarge, I want to see you."

Sarge lets go of my hands, and I know he is wrapping it around his hard cock. My mouth salivates at the thought. His eyes roll back in his head as I watch, my own orgasm building. The bed rocks as Enzo thrusts hard, his hand on Sarge's back pushing him down into the mattress. One of his legs steps up onto the ledge of the bed to change position.

"I'm going to come," Sarge says, and I let myself feel the vibrations against my clit. I shift so the vibrator is not only on my clit, but it's sitting just above my hole, wishing Killian's cock was buried deep inside me. He adds a third finger, and I feel every nerve ending in my body explode.

"Holy fucking shit!" I scream as my orgasm takes hold of me and keeps coming in wave after wave, and embarrassment washes over me when I feel myself let go. Killian's fingers quickly leave my ass, and his head comes underneath me, pulling me down, his lips suctioning over my pussy as he sucks every last drop from me.

My legs feel like jelly, and I drop down onto the bed. Killian places kisses down my spine, and Enzo rests his body against Sarge's.

"I need you to roll on your back and spread your legs."

Enzo and Sarge push up off the bed and head into the ensuite to shower, and Killian helps me roll onto my back, and I spread my legs like he asked. He wraps his hand around his cock and firmly grips it, and I watch with rapt attention at the way his hand slides up and down as he kneels on the bed in front of me. I push up on my elbows, watching and waiting as his breathing grows heavier and his strokes become faster until a jet of cum spurts onto my pussy. He falls forward, trapping me between his arms, placing a swift kiss on my lips before he rubs his cum into my skin.

"I love you, Poppet."

"I love you too, Killian. So much so it hurts. I never imagined that I could love three men as much as I do. You all complete me."

"I love you too," Sarge says, stepping out of the ensuite naked. "I never imagined I would ever love someone again after Missy, but I'm so glad I gave us a chance."

"Are we throwing around the L word?" Enzo asks. He is also still naked, but he runs a towel over his head. He comes to my side and sits down beside me.

"I know we had a different start to our relationship, and it's not traditional, but fuck if I don't love you. I think you stirred something in me from day one when you cried, and Sarge pulled his gun on me."

Killian tilts his head; this must be the first time that he is hearing about this. Enzo replays the story, and we all laugh. I still don't understand why he came back after paying a girl for sex and her crying. He definitely didn't get what he paid for.

"Great, we all love each other. Who is hungry?" Killian asks, pulling on a pair of sweats and a black shirt.

"I could eat," Sarge says.

We all get dressed and head downstairs. I pop my head in on Mario, and he has Mars in his baby swing, singing to him in Italian. He looks back and smiles at me.

"We are having a bite to eat; I can take him now if you want to go home."

"I'm fine, go eat and come get him before you head upstairs."

"You're an amazing Nonno, thank you."

He beams at me; he loves Mars so much and always wants to be around him. It melts my heart that my son is surrounded by people who love him, and he can have all the things I didn't get. My mom messages me every day to ask how he is. We are slowly building our relationship. Nothing will be able to take away the hurt, but every day is a small step in the right direction.

Mars stirs, and Mario shoos me away. I leave him to it and go back to the kitchen where Sarge has pulled out steaks, and Killian is chopping potatoes into fries. If this is how the rest of my life goes, I'm going to be a very happy woman. I have everything I need in this house right now, and I have never felt so safe, secure, and loved by my family.

CHAPTER TWENTY-EIGHT

JORDYN

With the baby monitor firmly in my hands, I head downstairs. Mars is finally on an amazing sleep schedule. The closer I get to Enzo's office, I can hear voices and angry ones. I push the door open, and Enzo and Mario are both speaking in Italian, hands flying around in the air. Clearing my throat, both men turn my way.

"Can you talk some sense into my son? Mars needs to be baptized, everyone in our family is."

Enzo laughs. "A fat lot of good that did us. We kill people. We all have a one-way ticket to hell. You might want to start getting on a first-name basis with the devil. There is no amount of praying that will save your soul."

"That's not the point."

I go to Enzo's side and wrap one arm around him. "I think we should do it. I know it means a lot to the family, and your aunts have been calling me every day to ask what I think."

Enzo's jaw goes hard. "Fine. But you can organize the whole thing, and I will just turn up. I wouldn't be surprised if the church bursts into flames when we all walk in, and I'm not hiding my relationship. Aunt Agnese can keep her mouth closed, or she doesn't come. She fucking calls me once a week to tell me she is praying for me. If I want to fuck men, I will."

Another throat clears. "If you're fucking men, I might have a problem with that, man. You're fucking a man. Did you tell her we use Jordyn as the meat in our sandwich every now and again?"

Mario chokes on air and pats himself on the chest. "You will all be the actual death of me. Let me take the baby monitor. I want to see my mini-me before I leave. Angelo and I will be gone for a few weeks; I'm taking him to introduce him to some connections that we have."

"Good. He needs to learn fast. I don't want to hold his hand forever."

Mario holds his hand out for the baby monitor. "We will be fine, but don't you have a party to go to today?"

Enzo goes still beside me. This party has been a sore spot for Enzo for a few weeks now. Killian was invited to his nieces' birthday party. He and Ronan have been keeping in contact. I agreed to go with him, but Enzo was dead set that Mars wasn't allowed to go. Which caused a huge argument that led to makeup sex. In the end, we talked it through, all four of us, and agreed that enemy territory is not a safe place for a baby.

I still wanted to go to support Killian. When the truth came out about the twins being Darragh's, Harper struggled a lot. Darragh was the hard egg to crack, apparently, but he has taken the girls in and treats them like princesses. Harper called me in a real state, trying to organize their birthday party. She panicked so badly, just wanting the day to be perfect. I don't exactly know what's going on with her, but every time I speak to her, she seems happy, and that's all I want for her.

"Okay, I'm going to get ready, Mars is asleep and should wake up in about an hour. Don't forget Sarge is going to see Missy today with Mars, so why don't you find something to do? I'm sure Mercedes could use your help at work. She told me you had a meeting today."

Enzo takes my hand and pulls me back into his body. "Since when do you talk to my personal assistant?"

"We both know she has a lady boner for me and just likes me better than you."

Enzo smirks and shakes his head. "Go get ready. And tell Mercedes I'm the fucking boss and will be in when I get there."

I head upstairs, and Sarge is in our bathroom getting dressed after showering. "Hey, how are you feeling?" I ask him.

He tips his lips and shrugs. "It shouldn't be this hard after all these years."

Stepping forward, I take his hand in mine and make him step forward. "It's the anniversary of her death. You're allowed to be sad, Sarge; she was a big part of your life. I want you to remember her, to celebrate her life. I actually got you something."

Dragging him out of the ensuite, I make him sit on the bed, and I retrieve the gift I hid in my underwear drawer, which means Killian knew about the gift. He snoops in my underwear and leaves the pair he likes sitting on top.

Nerves bundle in my stomach as I take it to him. He takes it from me and rips the gift paper off.

"I know it's weird to give it to you on this date, but I think you need it."

Tears well in his eyes as he looks down at the two small picture frames. Both have the same picture in it.

"There is one for downstairs where we have all the frames of family, and the other is for Mars's room. I want you to be able to tell him about her as he grows up."

"Thank you," he whispers. "They are perfect. Are you sure you're okay with me taking Mars with me?"

I nod. "As long as Kaser is with you. I know everything has been good, but we still can't be too careful when it comes to him."

"Of course. And how pissed is Enzo about you going to party it up with the Irish?"

I giggle. "He will get over it, he could have come if he wanted to. There is no bad blood between them, and I think they make good allies. I know what is at risk if something goes down, but my best friend is with them, and Killian will never admit it, but he likes the idea of family. He would never betray Enzo, and I think that is Enzo's fear that Killian will leave us."

"I would put a bullet in the Irish bastard's head before I ever left my family. He gave me a fucking guilt trip that the girls want to see me. I'm their only connection to their mother since Pike has no intention of coming back, and as much as I hated my sister, having Mars made me realize that the girls need to know their roots. I don't have much to tell them, but maybe helping them with their monsters is the least I can do," Killian says as he joins us in the room. Who knows how long he was standing outside the door. He goes into the walk-in closet and comes out with two gift bags.

"What did you end up getting them?" I ask. I left the gift buying up to him with the condition that it wasn't sharp or pointy.

"Monster repellant. Ronan says they still have nightmares about monsters."

Sarge laughs.

"What's so funny?" Killian asks him.

"You, you're this big bad guy, whose job for the 'Mafia'," Sarge uses air quotes when he says Mafia, which is a dig at me, "is torturing people, and you made them sweet little girls monster spray. It's adorable."

"Is not," Killian says with a pout.

I slap Sarge on the arm. "Stop teasing him or he will end up killing two people today to make up for it, and I don't want to be a witness to that today."

Stripping down, I pull on a sundress and let my hair down. "Mars is asleep in his nursery; Mario has the baby monitor. Wait until he wakes up and feed him before you take him out of the house. I have his baby bag packed and ready for you."

"Thank you," Sarge says from behind me as he wraps his arms around my middle and places a kiss on top of my head.

"Have fun today, and don't worry about Mars or Enzo, they will both be fine. Just make sure Kill is with you at all times. The Irish may have helped us once, but we still can't forget who they are."

"You know I will be safe. I have too much to lose now. Is

that what you're wearing?" I ask Killian with a raised brow. He looks down at his clothes and nods. I don't push him, it's a miracle that he is even going to this get-together slash party when there will be faces from the past there. People he knows exist, but he has never met. I'm just excited to get to be part of my best friend's world for a little while.

CHAPTER TWENTY-NINE

SARGE

Visiting Missy's grave is not something I do often. But now I have accepted that she is gone and never coming back. I don't feel the need to go every other day to talk to her. There are still days I miss her more than anything, and Jordyn will hold me, or we will talk about her. I love how accepting she is of my past. I don't know how I managed to get so lucky because most women would be jealous or feel a certain way, but not my Jordyn, she is perfect for me.

Pulling Mars's car seat from the SUV, Kaser stands at my side. Missy's parents, Susan and Mike, are here. Things after her death were not always great between us, and I understand why. My brother's lifestyle is the reason she isn't here. Now that I have Mars, I can understand why they felt the way they did. I couldn't imagine losing him. The thought alone causes a lump in my throat.

Sucking in a big breath, I take a step toward her grave. One step in front of the other until I'm standing beside Jeremy, her younger brother.

"I'll just be standing over by the tree if you need me."

Nodding, Kaser goes to stand just away from us to give me privacy, and I appreciate it.

"Sarge, we are glad you could come," Mike says.

"Oh my gosh, is that the baby?" Susan asks, as her eyes light up like it's Christmas. She knew how much Missy and I wanted to have a baby of our own.

"Yes, Mars."

Just as I say his name, he starts to stir; I place his car seat on the ground and bend down to unclip him. He looks so damn cute in his little khaki-colored pants and blue button-up shirt. Jordyn wanted him to look sharp the first time he met Missy.

"Can I hold him?" she asks, and I nod, handing him to her, and she cradles him to her chest. She knows my situation; we exchange messages every other week, and she updates me on the work that she does for the church and how Jeremy is doing in college.

"He is so precious; Missy would have loved him so much. She always had a way with babies."

I smile at the memory of Missy anytime she was around children; the excitement would light up her face.

"She would be so proud of you," Mike says.

Tears well in my eyes. "Thank you. My girlfriend printed a picture of Missy for his nursery, I can't wait until he is old enough to tell him stories about her."

Tears roll down Susan's face. "That was so thoughtful of her. I would love to meet her one day. It sounds like you have found yourself a good woman."

"The best," I say.

We all sit around Missy's grave for the next two hours,

reminiscing over all the fond memories we have of Missy and eating a lovely picnic that Susan packed. When I have to pack up and leave, I feel Missy here with me, her hands wrapped around my waist and her head resting against my back, telling me that she is glad that I'm happy, and I get this sense that she is responsible for sending Jordyn to me; that she knew I needed someone in my life.

Kaser pulls into the driveway of the house. Jordyn, Killian, and Pixie will still be at the party, and Enzo is probably at the club with a very shitty attitude. Unclipping Mars, I take him inside and up to our wing. When I get to the top step, the smell that comes from him is inhuman. Lifting him, I can see why. It's all the way up the back of his suit; he is more shit than baby. I am not prepared for a moment like this. I kick off my shoes and cradle him and his crap in my arms, turning on the shower. Once it's at the right temperature, I step in and slide down the wall, sitting Mars on my legs, careful to not let the water hit him in the face. I undo his clothes and throw them aside, and once his diaper is off, I set it outside the shower on the mat that will now go into the trash. While he rests on my legs, I remove my shirt and stand, cradling him against my chest, unclipping my jeans, and sliding them down my legs before rinsing Mars down.

"Sarge," Enzo calls out. "You up here?"

"In the shower, Mars had a blowout and Jordyn wasn't here to show me what to do."

Enzo steps into the bathroom and loosens his tie, watching me with desire in his eyes. Fuck, the way he looks at me has my whole body on fire. He grabs a towel from the rack and moves the bathmat aside. I slowly place his son in his arms, and he wraps him up. Mars smiles at him, and my heart swells. Fuck, I'm a sappy bastard.

"How did today go?" he asks as I step out in just my boxer briefs, sliding them down my legs before grabbing my own towel.

"Great, I finally think I'm okay. Content. I thought about calling my brother."

I haven't spoken to him in a long time. I needed someone to blame, and even when I no longer blamed him, maybe a part of me still did.

"If that is what you want to do, I will stand by you. Why don't you make the call while I dress Mars before he pisses all over me?"

I laugh. It wouldn't be the first or second time he has pissed on Enzo. Jordyn tries to tell him to place a wipe over his private area so he doesn't get covered, but Enzo is a hands-on learner, and the hard way is just how he learns.

Enzo leaves and takes Mars into the nursery. I get my phone from the diaper bag and sit on the bed, bringing up my brother's number. Before I can change my mind, I hit dial.

It almost rings out when I hear my brother's voice. "Sarge?"

It comes out like a question. "Yeah, it's me."

We sit in silence for a minute before he says anything. "How are you? I mean, I have thought about this moment and run things through my head, but nothing really seems to fit the moment."

"I'm good. I have a girl and a son now, well, he isn't biologically mine, but he is mine."

"What's his name?" he asks, and I can hear the smile on

his face. I know my brother all too well, he and Missy would talk babies together, which you would never expect coming from him based on the way he looks.

"Mars, he is Enzo's son, but we..."

"You don't have to explain yourself to me, I could always see something between you two, a spark."

I laugh, I never thought it was obvious, and back then, I would never have even considered a relationship like I have now. "Yeah, we are both in a relationship with Mars's mom and another guy. Enzo and I also are together."

"The perfect relationship. I wish I had the balls to do it. Lissa left me," he says, and that shocks me. "She wanted me to choose her or the guys. If it was as simple as she thought, I would have left."

"That sucks."

He chuckles. "That's an understatement. I only get to see my kids every other weekend. She only lets me stay at the house with them, and she goes to her parents."

We spend half an hour talking and catching up. I end the call telling him not to be a stranger, and I guess that goes both ways. I'm not ready to see him yet. Maybe one day I will be, but for now, I'm happy to start building a relationship with him again.

CHAPTER THIRTY

KILLIAN

The day has finally come. Jordyn doesn't know yet, but I have it all set up and ready to go. She promised me I could chain her up and do whatever I wanted with her and actually fuck her this time. The ice dildo is even making an appearance.

Mario is here for his play date with Mars. When he comes, he doesn't leave until we practically push him out of the door, so today he has agreed to stay until we are done. I didn't specifically tell him what we were doing.

With everything in place, I take the blindfold upstairs. Jordyn has started working out in the afternoons when Mario gets here, Enzo will be at the club for a little while, and Sarge went along with him. I have timed it so that we get our alone time to play, but they will be back to get their fill. If they want it after what I have planned for her. Knowing Sarge, he will unhook her and take her upstairs, and Enzo will blow his damn load at the thought of eating her out while she is full of cum. It's his thing, and who am I to judge when the thought of her tied up and bleeding for me has me ready to burst into my jeans.

The house is quiet for once, too. Pixie is out with Charlotte, spending up big on Enzo's credit card. She was more than happy to take off when I told her she had no limit today. Heading toward the gym, I hear the light sound of music as I push through the doors. Jordyn has a personal trainer, Danny, and the way his hand sits on her lower back as she does a stretch has me reconsidering taking her to the basement. He might need a lesson in keeping his hands to him fucking self.

Clearing my throat, poor Danny looks like he has seen a ghost and jumps a mile away from Jordyn. I smirk that my sheer presence is enough to almost make him piss his pants.

Jordyn shakes her head at me and says goodbye to Danny, then she walks over, her body covered in sweat.

"Why are you down here, Killian? We agreed that you stayed upstairs, you are not allowed to kill Danny, and he is more likely to suck Enzo's cock over being sexually attracted to me."

She throws her arms around my neck. "I have a surprise for you, so Danny can keep his hands for another day."

"Let me shower, and I'm all yours."

That makes me smile. It's sweet that she thinks I want her to shower. "Poppet, there will be no showering. You will wash away the flavor."

She grimaces and shakes her head at me. Untangling her hands from my neck, I pull the blindfold from my back pocket and tie it around her eyes.

"Now what?" she asks when it's securely in place. I circle her without replying, coming up behind her slowly so she can smell me, feel me behind her first. The hairs on the back of her neck stand on end when my lips near her ear. "Now, Poppet, I'm taking you downstairs."

A shiver washes over her. "Yes, please," she whispers.

I waste no more time here or we won't make it downstairs. Turning her, she easily follows my direction, and I throw her over my shoulder.

"Killian," she giggles, "You're going to drop me. I'm heavier than I was before Mars."

As I bring my hand down hard on her ass, she squeals, and I relish in the wobble of her cheeks under my hand, grabbing a handful and squeezing.

"How many times do I have to tell you that you're perfect? Every single curve makes me hard."

She pffts me. Since having Mars, she hasn't dropped the baby weight, not that I give a flying fuck, but apparently she is a little self-conscience about it.

I don't argue with her, not when I'm about to show her what her body does to me. Does she not know by now that I love an ass I can spread apart with my hands and squeeze while I eat her from behind, or knowing I could straddle her waist and put my cock between her tits and fuck them? Or that when she hugs me from behind—even though the very thought of being touched makes me want to lash out—when the softness of her body presses against me, it melts away that feeling, and I don't seem to care as much.

We cross paths with Mario. Jordyn can't see him, but he shakes his head at me and gives me a thumbs up.

"Tell the two bozos when they get home where to find us."

Mario laughs. "Killian," Jordyn chastises. "You did not

just tell my father-in-law in not so many words that you're dragging me into the basement."

I chuckle. "It's not the first time, and it won't be the last. We have needs, and Mario is a great babysitter we can trust."

The anticipation of having her downstairs makes me walk a little faster until I'm closing the basement door behind us so no one accidentally comes downstairs. I would hate to have to kill Milo for seeing my girl naked.

Placing her down on her feet, she waits. "Now, Poppet, safe words are not for me, so if I start going too far, I have made you an emergency device. I want you to hold it between your hands while I bind them, and only press down on the button if you need me to stop. It will bring the entire security team downstairs. If that happens, they have been told to shoot to kill."

"You won't hurt me, Killian."

Silly, silly girl, I can control myself around her, but what if I black out? It hasn't happened with her, but because of her, I won't take any chances. I maneuver her hands around the device and then bind them together before I add the chains. Once everything is in place, I connect her to the hook and wind it up until her toes barely touch the ground.

"I want you to focus on everything surrounding you, the sound of my voice, the way my hands feel against your skin." She nods. Pulling out my switchblade, the only sound in the room is the sound of the click it makes when I open it. I don't plan to hurt her much today, I want to see her bleed for me, just a little while I fuck her, get her ready, and hope Enzo and Sarge will play along. It's a fifty-fifty chance when it comes to Sarge. He likes to be the savior.

Bringing the blade to her neck, I run the tip along the

artery, knowing that one small slip could be disastrous. The trust she has in me doesn't go unnoticed, her chest rises and falls the closer the sharp tip gets to her chest, her large full breasts, and her large erect nipples. She shivers as I slow at her scar, one I have opened before.

"Do it, make it yours," she says. The first time was to open old wounds, to break her down, but this time she wants me to own her.

Pressing a little harder, watching as the skin splits apart and the first drop of blood forms has me grip the handle tighter, my self-control tested. All I want to do is dig it deeper, so instead of rolling down her cleavage, it drips beneath her feet.

Dipping the tip of the blade in her blood, I drag it down to the top of her sports bra, slicing the material. Her tits are huge now that she breastfeeds, and when the material gives, they explode from their confines. Leaning in, I lick the trail of blood back up to the small cut on her skin, and she shivers beneath me. Kissing back down towards her navel, goosebumps line her skin. I want to take my time, but every bone in my body aches with need, to sink so deep inside her.

Placing the blade on the floor, I hook my fingers into the waistband of her spandex leggings, slowly sliding the material over the swell of her hips, which are a little more pronounced after giving birth. With my thumbs securely inside the material, I let the rest of my calloused hand run down her silky soft skin, digging my nails into her flesh when I stop just under her milky white thighs. Knowing the crescent shape will bruise well after we finish.

I want her to feel me everywhere, her pussy begging me,

the scent of her arousal thick in the air before I touch her in the places she will beg me to touch. A breath of air lightly against her perfect cunt has her whimper and thrust her hips forward.

"You need to stay still, Poppet, or I will punish you for your bad behavior."

"Yes, please," she whispers, "Punish me, Killian."

My name on my lips doesn't help my case, it makes me want to shove my cock down her throat, gagging on it while her spit rolls down her chin and her eyes water before turning into tears.

Pushing to my feet, I walk over to the freezer and pull out one of the ice dildos I made last night. Pressing the ice to her back, she pulls in a lung full of air, not expecting how cold it is. Moving it, I trace the outline of my name that is forever etched into her skin. She moves against her restraints as I drag it down her spine, one vertebra at a time, until I reach the top of her ass. She knows where this is leading, and I made sure to not make it all that big for her first time. I want to stretch her ass so when Enzo and Sarge get here, they can double up and fuck her together.

When I get to her crack, she sucks her ass in, but that won't help her. I try to refrain from talking to her since she tells me all of the time that I could bring her to climax just by talking.

Pressing a light kiss on her shoulder, I bring the ice to her back entrance, pushing it so light it won't go inside her, just enough to get her used to the feeling.

"Fuck, I need you," she cries.

Biting down on her shoulder, she screams as my teeth break the skin, and I push what's left of the ice inside her.

"Oh shit, it's so cold, you need to feel this, please," she begs.

Coming around to her front, I pick up my blade, running it up the inside of her left leg, grazing it over an old scar. One that makes me livid every time I see it, knowing another man dared to mark her so close to her pussy, thinking he marked her for life. What sick, twisted pleasure he got from it. I destroy it by opening it up and watching the blood drip down her skin.

With every ounce of self-restraint I have, I throw the knife far enough away from me. The thoughts of hurting her flood through my brain, knowing the only way to turn it off is to strip out of my clothes, something that will surely change where my brain is going. Slipping my fingers inside her pussy unexpectedly has her crying out my name. I can feel how cold she is, and fuck hurting her, fucking drawing it out, I need her pussy. Removing my fingers, I suck them into my mouth, savoring the taste on my tongue.

"Fuck, you taste so sweet," I tell her. She shivers with a whimper.

My cock is hard as a rock. I run my hand over the blood dripping down her leg; it's not enough to be concerned that she is losing too much blood. I have drained many men to the brink of death, and I'm confident that she will be fine.

With my hand fully coated, I wrap it around my cock, stroking it a few times, covering it with her, knowing I'm about to be balls deep inside her.

"I hope that pussy is ready for me." The only warning she will get. Moving closer, so close her body presses against mine, she tries to pull back. She knows to not push me too quickly, but I wrap my hand around her back and pull her close to me. I need her blood and the way it feels between our bodies. Knowing that with each thrust when I'm inside her, the thick substance gluing us together is all her.

"Killian, please, I need you."

My cock presses against her pussy, and she wraps her legs around my waist. I should slap her away—she isn't in charge of this, I am. But I don't, I need her as much as she needs me.

I remove the blindfold just as I thrust inside her, needing to see her face as I bury myself in the one place I belong.

"Fuck!" she screams. Her pussy strangles me, every one of her muscles clenching around me. When she opens her eyes, they take me in.

"You're covered in blood," she whispers, and I nod. Fucking oath I am. Sweeping the hair out of her face with one hand while the other stays firmly under her ass, she starts to grind against my cock.

"You look beautiful covered in red." She moans as I thrust. I want to take her from behind, suspended from the ceiling, but I will wait until her stomach muscles are up to it. From this angle, I can control and hold her weight. "Your pussy is so tight."

"No, your cock is huge," she says, and I lean in and nip at one of her nipples, knowing she doesn't want us to suck them.

"Oh, fuck," she gasps, her head falling back. I pound inside her faster and faster, chasing my relief as her soft moans become louder and louder.

Movement catches my eye. I was so caught up in the moment I didn't hear the door. Enzo already has his shirt off ready to join in, and Sarge stands off to the side, his jaw tight.

I won't be surprised if he tries to smack me in the mouth when I'm done.

"Fuck, Killian, I'm going to come," she cries, and before she gets a chance to come, I spill my load deep inside her. It may be an asshole move, but I know Enzo will want her juices dripping from his chin. I step back, and she opens her eyes, blinking a few times, and notices Enzo now directly in front of her. Pushing his way in front of me, he squats down in front of her, wrapping his arms around her behind and pulling her into his face.

I leave him to it, and her cries of pleasure fill the air. Sarge still looks torn. "Embrace it, Sarge, she wants this. Go get your cock out because she wants you to fuck her in the ass while Enzo takes her pretty pussy. You know you want it."

He pushes off the wall and throws a right hook in my face. I smirk at him; I knew it would happen. "That's for hurting her, asshole."

"Worth it," I laugh. He walks over to her, stripping off his clothes as he goes, his cock already rock hard. Fucking liar is just as turned on as I am.

Enzo eats her cunt like he is starved, his face buried so far into her as she screams his name. I love that she is a squirter, her juices cover him so much so that when he stands, he wipes his hand down his face and flicks his hand. He removes the rest of his clothes, and Sarge helps her wrap her legs around him. I move back closer and lower her chains a little so they can move her into a better position. Sarge reaches under her and slides his fingers through her wetness before inserting a finger in her ass, and I position myself so I can see everything. The way Enzo's cock slides inside her, and Sarge adding a second finger and pumping them, stretching her out. To when he pulls his fingers out, steps up behind her, and bends his knees to line himself up. My dick stirs to life again as I wrap my hand around the base, slowly sliding up to the tip and down again.

"I'm so full," she cries.

"You can take it," I tell her. "You were made just for us. Just relax, feel the way their cocks touch separated by a thin wall of skin."

Her head falls back, and Sarge kisses the side of her face and whispers something to her. Both men fall into a rhythm as her body relaxes. Even my strokes match theirs, and we each draw every last ounce of pleasure from not only ourselves but her before I come into my hand as she screams, her body shuddering and going limp. Sarge growls and holds her waist as he comes, and when he slides out of her, Enzo pulls her in closer, and within a few thrusts, he finishes inside her. She clings to him, and I help move the chains. He hands her to Sarge, who cradles her in his arms. It's him that needs aftercare right now as much as she does.

Enzo slides his pants back on and tells me he will make sure his father is out of sight while we take her upstairs and run a bath.

We do just that, take her upstairs and bathe her, clean her small wounds, and show her how much we love her.

EPILOGUE

JORDYN

Mars's second birthday

Mario is crazy. What two-year-old needs a party this big? He insists on the best for his grandson, so there are face painters, bouncy houses, a petting zoo, and clowns. You name it, it's here.

Mercedes walks down the side of the house with her girlfriend by her side. I smile at them, and she waves. Enzo gave in and made her the manager of the club so he could step back from those duties. His not so legal activities take up a lot of his time, and he still has issues handing some of the responsibility to Angelo, and I can see why as Angelo comes running past me with Mars securely in his arms. He pauses quickly and looks at me.

"If Aunt Maria asks, you haven't seen us; the woman is crazy. She has no boundaries, even when I told her that she has to ask Mars if he wants a kiss."

I shake my head. Mars hates forced love and the aunts

are over-affectionate. Angelo has taken it upon himself to be Mars's personal aunt repellent at parties.

"Take him to the petting zoo. Aunt Maria hates ducks, and there is one in there. Just make sure to watch him."

Angelo nods and places a kiss on my cheek. I never in a million years thought that Angelo and I would be on good terms, but he has spent the last two years proving himself. It's only his brother left to convince.

Sarge comes up behind me and wraps his arms around my growing stomach. He finally convinced me to do this one more time, and reluctantly, I agreed. I'm thankful Killian doesn't want biological children. When I got pregnant with Michelle or Misha for short, because using Missy felt wrong to me—Missy plays a huge part in our lives—Killian sat me down with a serious look on his face. My stomach sank, and I thought for a second that he would ask for a child of his own, but it was the opposite. He doesn't want to continue his family name; he sat me down and he confessed he had a vasectomy when he turned thirty. He never wanted children of his own, and he still doesn't. He is happy with the family we have created.

"How is my beautiful wife and daughter?"

Yes, wife, even if it's not legal. We had a very small ceremony in the backyard, just us, Pixie, Harper, Mario, Angelo, and Missy's family. Which may seem weird to others, but since the day Sarge took Mars to meet her family, they have been a constant in my son's life. He calls them Nanna and Poppa, and they treat him as if he is their own.

My relationship with my mother is healed. She and Cal are actually married now, living their best free-spirited life.

They couldn't make it today; they are in Australia on their honeymoon. I'm happy for her.

Killian comes out of the back sliding door with Pixie hot on his heels. Her fun-loving teen style has transformed into a goth era...maybe. She is dressed head to toe in black, along with heavy eyeliner. She has been pestering Killian to let Milo teach her what he knows. I have enforced a rule that she isn't allowed back down in that basement until she is sixteen, which is only a week away, and it makes me nervous. My little sister is bloodthirsty, and nothing I say or do is going to change that. I'm not an idiot. I know she fights; the bruises she comes home with make it very clear, and Milo let slip that she has been training and likes to kick ass. Which is on my list of things I want to tell Enzo, but really don't need a war to start with the Aces crew. Things have been quiet, and it's the way I like it. None of the families are at war, there is an understanding between us.

"We are good, just standing here wondering how I got so lucky."

Misha kicks Sarge's hand, and he laughs. She loves the sound of his voice. "I'm the lucky one. Thank you."

I turn to face him and wrap my arms around his neck. "You don't have to thank me; I love you more than you know."

Sarge looks over my shoulder, and I feel someone step up to my back. "Do you think we could sneak away?"

"Enzo, it is your son's birthday party, there will be no sneaking," I say with a laugh.

"I don't know," Killian says, coming to stand beside us. "I doubt anyone would know that we are gone."

"Oh no," Harper says, coming up beside us and grabbing

my arm, pulling me out from between my men. "I know that look, and nothing good can come from it."

"Plenty good comes from it. I don't know what those Irish fucks are doing, but it must not be right," Killian says, and Harper scoffs.

"You forget my former career, I know what I'm doing," Harper says and winks at my guys as she drags me away. "It's almost time for cake. Mario was going to get it set up."

"Thank you, I have no self-control around those men, they make me weak."

Harper laughs. "I know that feeling."

We both go in search of Mars, and we find him and Angelo in the petting zoo. Angelo has the freakin' duck tucked under one arm as he chases my son around.

"Why is he carrying a duck?" Harper asks.

"Because Aunt Maria is afraid of them."

Mars comes running towards us and beelines straight for Harper. She leans over the cage and plucks him up into her arms.

"How's my favorite nephew? Are you ready to eat some cake?"

Mars giggles and claps his hands. "Cake, Cake," he parrots her.

Just as we turn around, Mario is bringing out a cake on a damn cart. It's so big he has to push it outside.

"Where is Mars?" he shouts and scans the area. Harper hands him to me, and I take him up to his Nonno. He practically launches himself out of my arms.

My three men come and stand by my side, and we all sing happy birthday to the miracle that brought us all together and changed our lives for the better.

It all feels like it was yesterday, Enzo walking into the brothel and choosing me, the tears through our first session. The heartbreak when I left and they didn't come for me, finding out I was pregnant and hating the fact I was bringing life into this world to going back to them. Now, I'm happier than I ever thought was possible with family and friends by my side.

HARPER

I always knew growing up that I would have to fight for what I want, and I would have to protect myself. Huntersville is not a place where you get your happy ever after. The men here are not even villains, they are the scum of the earth, watching and waiting for you to show an ounce of vulnerability.

Taking control of my life, I started working at The Range when I was eighteen. Being a whore in a brothel wasn't what I wanted in life, but I figured out really fucking fast that girls like me don't get what they want.

Owning my sexuality is important to me. Some may not agree with selling your body, but why the fuck not? Men like what they see, and they can pay for my time. That is until it was all ripped away from me in the blink of an eye. Men came into my safe place and took from me, the one thing I guarded sacred, the one thing all the women here had, the right over their own body, no man to tell us what to do.

Because I'm a whore, they thought they had a right to take, to strip me down and force themselves on me. Now each time I look in the mirror, I don't see the woman I once was, I see the shame that I couldn't protect myself, and every time I close my eyes, I hear the sound of the girls screaming, and furniture breaking.

But my best friend won't let me be a victim, she prefers to be seen as a survivor of the horrors of the world. Maybe she is right, since there are no men riding in on white horses to save the day. Nah, the men who want to save me come in Jeeps, with combat boots and accents that melt my fucking panties off. They are not the type who hold your hand and guide you to your feet; no, they're the type who grab you by the hair and drag you to your feet and whisper all the messed-up shit they want to do to you, throw you over their shoulder, slap your ass, and call you a good girl.

I wish my story was as easy as that. I might come across as a woman who knows what she wants, but I'm also very similar to that of a feral cat. If you get too fucking close, I will scratch your eyes out and hiss at you. Except a feral cat won't stop the Irish Mafia. They don't thrive on obedience like some would like to think. They enjoy the chase and they have me set in their sights.

They take what they want, and it might seem like I go willingly, but that can't be further from the truth. They want the real me back, but that girl is long gone, the one with the fake smile and bubbly personality. They won't stop until they find her, and she is buried under the men who hurt me. Every time I run, one of them is there to catch me.

They warned me that they would also be close by, I just never realized how much I liked to be chased.

I'm Harper Lou Daniels, and I have been a bad girl; I wonder who will catch me first.

. . .

Here's to hell! May the stay there be as fun as the way there!

Acknowledgements

My husband, I love you.

My children, thank you for being hungry all of the time and forcing me to keep working.

To my best friend Amber, thank you for being a huge support for me both professionally and personally.

My alpha readers, Patricia, Cheria, Rachel, Lena, Istha, Kristin, without you ladies, I would be lost. You always jump straight in and get shit done, and I will be forever grateful.

Brandi, your proofreads always go above and beyond. Thank you for being a valuable part of my team.

My ARC readers, reviews are one of the most important parts of being an author and each and every one of you leaving reviews means so much more than you could ever know.

My street team girls, thank you so much for taking a chance on me and sharing my work.

And last but not least my readers, for giving my stories a chance and investing your time into loving my characters as much as I do. If it wasn't for you I wouldn't have a career doing something that I love.